Haunting Memories

Holly Huntress

This one is for all of those who have
supported me since the beginning.
Thank you.

Chapter One
Zac

A roaring siren rang in my ears. Opening my eyes, my vision was blurred, and my head pounded, like someone was stabbing my brain with a thousand needles. Words escaped me as I attempted to speak.

Blinking slowly, I tried to focus. I could make out Mom's brown, pixie-cut hair, and tear-filled hazel eyes as she walked alongside me. I laid vertically on some kind of... Stretcher. I was on a stretcher. *Why am I on a stretcher?*

The sirens faded and my mom's faint, trembling voice, asked, "What happened? Is he going to be okay?" Before it all went black.

"Zac."

My eyes fluttered open at the sound of Dad's voice.

"You're awake! We were so worried." Dad hugged me tightly, and I gasped in pain. He pulled back, an apologetic look on his face. "How do you feel?"

"I, uh, not so great. What happened?" I stretched my uninjured arm. The other was in a sling, and it ached anytime I so much as *thought* about moving it. The room around me was small with bare, white walls. Two chairs sat close to the bed for visitors and a TV was mounted on the wall opposite me. I itched at the IV in my arm and winced with each beep of the EKG machine. Clearly, I was in the hospital, but I had no idea why.

"We were hoping you could tell us that." Dad gripped the railing on the bed, his knuckles white. "Don't you remember anything?"

"No. The last thing I remember is going to the park with Ally." I scanned the room again, looking for her. "Where is she? Is she okay?"

Dad's face turned ghostly pale and his deep brown gaze dropped to the floor. Stepping away from the bed, he shoved a hand through his short, brown hair.

He mumbled something to himself and then said, "Josh stopped by earlier and I told him you needed some time, since you don't remember anything from that night. He promised to stop by the house when you're feeling better."

"Oh." My mind whirled.

"Here comes your mom." Dad waved to the door. "She's been anxious to speak with you." He seemed like he couldn't get out of the room fast enough as he hurried out the door.

Letting out a long sigh, I rubbed my head, noticing a bump on the side of it, which I guessed had something to do with my pounding headache.

"Oh, sweetie, you're finally awake!" Mom rushed over and hugged me, sending another stab of pain through my arm.

"Mom, where's Ally?" The look Dad gave me had struck a nerve, and I knew something was wrong.

Mom bit her lip and twirled the wedding ring on her finger. "You must be hungry," she said. "Let me go and get you some food, dear." She kissed my forehead and left almost as quickly as Dad had.

I tried to move but my vision swam, and a wave of dizziness hit me. The doctor walked in before I could attempt to move again.

"Good morning, Zachary." The doctor nodded to me. His name tag said, *Doctor Gray.* "How are you feeling today?"

"I have a headache, and shooting pains in my arm," I said. "I also can't remember anything from last night."

"Mm. We had a similar conversation when you came in, though I doubt you remember." I didn't. "You have a small fracture in your arm, and a large lump on your head, which I believe is why you can't remember anything from the incident. The combination of the blow to the head and the psychological trauma can cause such memory loss. It's called traumatic amnesia. There is no permanent damage, and it's possible your memories will come back. Maybe a little bit at a time, as the swelling decreases, but don't be worried if they don't." Dr. Gray finally looked up from his clipboard. "Any questions?"

Any questions? I had a million questions, but I wasn't about to go spewing them out to this random doctor I'd met mere seconds ago.

"How long has it been?" I asked instead of the hundreds of probably more important questions.

"Since you hit your head? You've only been in the hospital since last night. You woke up briefly when you first came in, but you were still in a state of shock from what we believe has caused your traumatic amnesia."

This all seemed very bizarre. How could I not remember what happened the night before?

"Anything else?" Dr. Gray asked, interrupting my stream of thought.

"No." I groaned as I shifted my weight in the bed and my whole body cringed from the movement.

Dr. Gray clutched his clipboard at his side and lowered his voice. "I've recommended to your parents that you see a therapist following your discharge from the hospital. I think it will help both with the recovery of your memories and dealing with the grief-"

"Grief?" Though I couldn't remember why, I realized the doctor was right. Deep down, a hollowness threatened to overwhelm me if I let it.

"Well, it's to be expected after what you experienced..." He trailed off and cocked his head to the side. "Have your parents told you yet?"

"Told me what?" I snapped. No one would be straight with me, and it hurt anytime I tried to remember what had happened last night.

"I'll let them tell you." Dr. Gray checked my IV and left the room.

There was a little commotion outside my room, and loud whispers that I couldn't quite make out.

"Please, ma'am, time is of the essence, if we could speak with him for a minute," a deep, rumbling voice spoke.

"I told you; he remembers nothing. It will only further upset his current state. Obviously, I care deeply about Ally, but—"

I shot upright, making pain shoot through my side, but I ignored it.

"Mom, what's going on?" I called, leaning forward enough to see two police officers standing outside my room. I locked eyes with one of them.

Mom waved her hand toward the door, caving to them and letting them enter. "These two officers want to ask you if you remember anything from last night, even though I've already told them you don't."

I curled my lip. "Why? What's going on?"

"I'm sorry I didn't get a chance to tell you sooner, but," Mom sighed. "Ally is missing, sweetie."

"Wha- how?" I could hardly comprehend how that could have happened. Last I remembered, we were walking to the park together.

A solid lump formed in my throat, and I thought I might throw up. There was no way I'd never see Ally again. They'd find her. They had to.

I could almost feel my memories of her being ripped away as mom kept talking and my head spun.

One of the officers stepped forward and spoke. "Which is why we're here. We need to know if there is anything you can remember after arriving at the park last night. Any small piece of information, even if you think it's unimportant, could help us immensely."

The room spun, and the walls seemed to be closing in as the lump in my throat made it harder and harder to breathe.

"Um." I tried clearing my throat. "No. I don't remember. There were other people at the park, but I can't remember who. Jake, Mariah, that's all I remember."

"That's a starting point," the officer said. "We hope to speak with you again once you're out of here."

Mom ushered them out.

"I need to get out of here." I stood but wobbled on my feet.

"Whoa, you have to wait until the doctor gives you the 'okay' to leave." Mom lightly pushed me back down onto the bed.

"Well, get him here fast. I need to get out of here."

Why can't I remember that night, I thought, as my vision narrowed. Thankfully, the doctor walked in.

After being discharged, I gathered my things. My reflection in the mirror startled me. My short brown hair stuck out in all different directions, and I attempted to smooth it down a bit to no avail. I was wheeled out of the hospital in a wheelchair.

Outside in the fresh air, I thought the claustrophobia would ease up, instead, the world came crashing down.

Ally was *missing*. She wouldn't be waiting for me when I got home. I wouldn't pass her in the halls at school.

What if it was me? What if I *had something to do with her going missing?* The thought hit me hard, knocking the breath from me. It would make sense why I blocked last night from my memories. I couldn't bear to think of hurting her.

No. Stop. I wouldn't hurt her.

I sat on the sidewalk and put my head between my knees while Dad went to get the car.

"Zac, I know this is a lot to take in, but I'm here if you need me," Mom said, but I barely heard her. A deafening roar filled my ears. She sat down beside me and put her arm around my shoulders. "She's only been missing less than a day, I'm sure she's fine."

Dad patted me on the back as he helped me into the car. "We're going to be all right," he reassured me, but I could hear the slight hitch in his voice.

He thinks you did it. Another intrusive thought. I gritted my teeth and ignored it.

At home, I moved mechanically through the house, counting the stairs as I climbed them to my room. It was like Ally and I had left it. The Uno cards were still scattered across the floor. I knelt to pick them up.

"Why can't I remember anything?" I asked myself, pushing all the cards into a pile and plopping them into the box. I shoved the game to the back of my closet. I couldn't look at it and be reminded every time of the night I barely remembered. Tears rolled down my cheeks as I forced myself to think back to the last memory I had of that night with Alana. It was October thirteenth. Three days ago.

"Hahaha! I win again!" Alana threw down her last card on the carpet.

"You cheated." I stuck my tongue out at her.

"No way! I'm a champion Uno player!" She giggled and stood up, holding her hand out to me. "Come on. Let's go somewhere."

I took her hand and let her pull me to my feet.

"Where?" I asked, kicking one of the uno cards to the side.

"The park?" she suggested. I had a feeling this wasn't a spur of the moment decision.

I sighed. "All right. We have to be back by nine though, school night and all that."

"That gives us two hours. Let's go!" Alana pulled me out into the hall.

"Whoa! Let me tell my parents I'm leaving first." I laughed. My parents were fine with us going to the park, which I hadn't been worried about.

Once we were out of the house, Ally skipped down the street, seeming like she was in a hurry.

"Why do we need to get there so fast?" I asked, speed walking to keep up with her.

She turned to me and smiled. "There may or may not be a bunch of other people already there." Her blue eyes glimmered as she revealed the truth.

"Oh." I deflated. "I thought this was... Well never mind." I avoided her pity-filled gaze.

"I know it's our night, but this will only be a quick thing, I promise. We can go back to your house at eight if you want." She fluttered her eyelashes.

"No, no. It's fine. Nine o'clock is good."

She squealed in excitement and hugged me. It was hard to say no to her.

"You are the BEST friend anyone could have." She raced toward the park, now only yards away. A group of people had already gathered there, all from our school. I weaved through them and climbed up the precarious wooden tower at

the center of the playground. I watched Ally mingle with all the people whom I'd never wanted to be friends with.

The last thing I remembered was seeing Ally laughing with someone. I couldn't put names to any of the faces I'd seen, it was as if they'd all been blurred out in my memory.

I punched my pillow.

"What happened to her?!" I flopped down on my bed, covering my face with a pillow.

"Honey, are you okay?" Mom called up the stairs.

"Fine!" I curled up and stayed like that until I fell asleep.

My dreams were filled with images of Ally crying out for help, or dying on the ground, and I could do nothing to help her. I woke up covered in sweat.

There was a light knock on my door.

"Zac," Dad said. "Can I come in?"

"Fine." I sighed.

He sat on the edge of my bed and neither of us said anything for a few minutes.

"Did they have a search party for her?" I asked.

He nodded. "They've been searching all day, but there aren't a lot of places to hide around here. Even the woods behind the park only go so far before you hit the next neighborhood. They scoured every inch of those woods and well, they did find some blood. But they're still testing it."

I bit my lip, trying to keep from screaming in frustration, and didn't stop even when I tasted my own blood.

Blood. They found blood.

"Can we-"

"Yeah. Put on a jacket and we'll go out with the search party tonight." Dad didn't even have to hear my question; he knew what I'd been about to ask. I needed to look for her myself. I needed to see where they'd found the blood and try to remember what had happened. No matter what.

Even if it turns out I'm the one who made her disappear, that small voice said.

Chapter Two

Alana

Two weeks before

I'd never felt more peaceful. Pressure pushed into me from every side, but instead of being claustrophobic, it made me warm and *comforted*. Until I realized I couldn't breathe. A nothingness so blindingly bright that it hurt my eyes, appeared above me and the pressure was gone. I squeezed my eyes shut, but the light penetrated my eyelids.

Is this heaven? I thought. Or was I dreaming?

Water streamed down onto the floor around me from some unknown source and I took a step toward the abyss. The ground fell out from under me, and I tumbled down. I was sinking to the bottom of a pool, and when I hit the bottom, I woke.

I shot up in bed. When I realized I was in my room, I let my head fall back to the pillow. The clock on my side table read five o'clock in the morning, but I couldn't fall back asleep. I lay awake, staring at the ceiling.

My phone beeped and I jumped.

Who else would wake up so early?

Jake's name scrawled across the illuminated screen, and I smiled.

Pressing the green answer button, I said quietly, "Hey babe, what's up?"

"Ally, baby!" He was clearly drunk. "I wanted to check in with ya!" There was snickering in the background, and I rolled my eyes. My momentary joy dissipating.

"Is this important Jake?" I tried to sound annoyed, though I was happy he'd called.

"Of course! When are calls from me not important? Any who, wanted to tell ya I can't hang out later." Jake hung up the phone.

Sighing, I placed my phone back in its place beside my pillow. We *had* made plans for that day, but apparently drinking with his friends was more important than keeping those plans. It happened all too often with him those days.

I covered my face with a pillow and screamed into it. After I was able to fall back asleep since Jake had thoroughly taken my mind away from my creepy dream.

I slept until noon, when someone banging around downstairs woke me. It wasn't often I slept that late. I rolled out of bed and fought with the door handle so I could go downstairs and investigate the noise.

"Good morning, sleepy head!" My mom's boyfriend Clyde's voice met me at the bottom of the stairs. He was in the kitchen opening and slamming what seemed to be all the cabinet doors.

"What are you doing?" I asked, rubbing the sleepiness from my eyes.

"I can't seem to find..." Clyde shot up with a bottle of whiskey in his hand. "A-ha! Here it is!" He uncapped the bottle and slugged it down. "It's been too long."

"Try, like, twelve hours," I grumbled. Clyde always needed a drink in his hand, no matter what time it was.

"No talking from you on this subject, try talking to me about it when you're thirty years older." Taking another swig,

Clyde went into the living room and slumped down onto the couch.

I grabbed a box of cereal from the cabinet and made my way back upstairs.

After an uneventful day of trying to contact Jake, even though he had cancelled our plans, I decided to call Mariah.

"Wanna hangout?" I asked her as I flopped down on my bed, letting out a huff.

"I thought you were hanging out with Jake today?" Mariah asked, with a hint of concern in her voice.

"Nah, he's busy." I rolled over onto my stomach, looking at the picture on my side table of me and Jake. It was taken the previous year, back when we were genuinely happy. In the picture, we were on the beach in the middle of fall, when we had first started dating. It was cloudy and rainy, and he twirled me around. I had blonde hair that reached the bottom of my shoulder blades.

Since then, I'd dyed my hair brown because of a lame attempt to change things up in my life. There was a spark of joy in my blue eyes, but I hadn't seen that in a while. Jake still had his cropped brown hair and hazel eyes. He stood about half a foot taller than me, and he had muscles that would make you think he went to the gym every day, which he did most days back then, but not so often anymore. He had sharper features, and his jaw was often tight because he never seemed to relax anymore. From the outside looking in, we seemed to be made for each other.

"That seems to be the case a lot these days." Mariah was always concerned about my relationship.

I traced my slightly round, but heart shaped face, in the picture, imagining what I'd look like with a bob cut.

Mariah meant well with her worrying, and Jake *could* be a little harsh sometimes, but it was those moments he was the sweetest, most charming boyfriend in the world that I lived for.

Besides, Mariah was being a hypocrite. Her relationship with Josh hadn't been all it was cracked up to be either, though they *had* broken up a few days ago.

"He needs some time with his friends," I defended Jake, like always. We'd been dating for a year; since the beginning of my sophomore year and his junior year. Now, he was less than a year away from graduating.

"So, I guess we should go shopping?" Mariah suggested.

My phone beeped with a text from Jake.

I'm coming to pick you up. We're going to dinner with Connor and Molly. I couldn't help but be excited he wanted to take me out to dinner with his friends.

"Actually, Jake texted me and said Connor and Molly want us to go out to dinner with them!" I gushed.

"Oh, okay. Well, I guess I'll talk to you later." Mariah hung up.

It was the first time all week Jake had asked *me* to hang out. He hadn't even answered my texts in two days, and now he wanted to go out to dinner. I was ecstatic. I was always the one pushing him to make plans.

Jake pulled up outside the house at six o'clock and honked his horn. Running downstairs, I yelled at my mom, Dianna, that I was leaving. I'd stopped referring to her as *mom* whenever I talked about her.

"All right. See you later," Dianna responded indifferently. We hardly ever spoke anymore.

Jake waited in the driveway in his jacked-up Chevy truck. His pride and joy. Jake backed out of the driveway, and we rode in silence to the restaurant. I knew not to confront him when he was quiet like that. He often didn't care to hear what I had to say anymore, and I didn't want to bore or annoy him.

When we pulled into the parking lot of the restaurant, Molly and Connor weren't there yet. Jake turned off his truck and angled himself toward me. I smiled at him, hoping he was in a good mood that night.

"What did you do today?" he asked.

I watched him and noticed the way he kept glancing out the windshield for his friends, like it was uncomfortable for him to be alone with me.

"Nothing. I hung out at home today," I answered.

"Good." Jake nodded slowly and continued. "I hung out with some people earlier. You know, like Connor, Joe and Katrina."

I smiled weakly. Katrina was his ex, and they'd been hanging out a lot lately. Supposedly with other people, but it didn't stop the doubts from creeping in. I never said anything, though, because I didn't want Jake to think I was jealous.

"Sounds fun," I said instead. The rest of the time was spent waiting in silence. All I could think about was what Jake had been doing with Katrina earlier.

Molly and Connor arrived, and we all went inside. I didn't know them very well; they were Jake's friends. Jake hardly ever asked me to hang out with him when he was with his friends, except for when he had parties.

We were seated at a table, though I knew Jake preferred booths. Across from us, there was a large mirror that covered the whole wall. It always made me think the restaurant was much bigger than it was.

I opened my menu and read all the different choices while Jake and Connor talked about some new truck that Connor had bought. I spaced out and didn't realize when Molly tried talking to me until Jake nudged my arm.

"Huh?" I looked up. Molly looking annoyed across the table.

"Molly was saying she likes your shirt," Jake said, raising his brows at me, he hated it when I spaced out.

It was a light blue, long-sleeved V-neck; nothing special. I tried to smile to ease the tension.

"Thank you. I got it for my birthday," I told her. Molly nodded and looked down at the menu. I'd only met her once at one of Jake's parties. She was one of those girls that was always hanging onto all the guys. I knew she didn't like me much.

My phone rang. I grabbed it from my purse and shut it off. Jake hated it when I texted or called anyone while I was with him, though he had no problem doing it himself. Before it turned off, I saw a text from Mariah.

"Sorry," I muttered, staring down at my menu until the waiter came.

Jake and Connor continued talking about things I didn't care about. Molly pretended to be engaged in their conversation so she wouldn't have to talk to me.

Connor smiled at me a few times, maybe trying to make me feel better about the awkward situation, but it helped nothing.

The night dragged on. We ate and lingered at our table for a little while longer than necessary. I picked at my nails. When we finally got up to leave, Molly decided she needed to go to the bathroom, and we had to wait for her to come back before leaving.

Once Jake and I were back in his truck, I breathed a sigh of relief.

"That was nice," I lied.

Jake started his truck and waved to Connor and Molly as we pulled out of the parking lot.

"Can't you at least *try* to like my friends?" he scowled. I didn't think I had done anything wrong. "This is why I never let you hang out with us."

"What are you talking about?" I asked incredulously.

"You were ignoring Molly the whole night."

"No, I wasn't. She was ignoring *me*. It's your friends who don't like me,"I tried to clarify.

He shook his head but dropped the subject. He put his arm out toward me, and I scooted over on the seat so he could drape his arm around my shoulders. I leaned my head on him.

"I'm sorry. I'm happy you came to dinner tonight," he admitted. I smiled; these were the moments that made me love him.

He pulled up outside my house, and I gazed up at him. Turning his head to me, he kissed my forehead. I didn't want to pull away from his warm and strong embrace.

"Call me later?" I asked.

He nodded and kissed me again. "Love you, babe."

I took that as my cue to leave and scooted away from him toward the door.

"Love you, too." I opened the car door and hopped out.

Inside the house, Dianna and Clyde were watching TV. When Dianna had tried to stop me from seeing Jake, I remembered thinking about how hypocritical she was being. Clyde wasn't exactly the most caring, loving person in the world either. Dianna had a 'reasonable' explanation, as she called it, for that. Apparently, Clyde grew up in the next town over with foster parents. Dianna told me they tried to love him, but Clyde rebelled and acted out at every chance he got. He started drinking when he was thirteen and after that, it was his new escape from life.

"Hey mom." I stood behind the couch and put my hand on her shoulder. Saying the word *mom* made me long for a time when she had acted like one for me. "I'm gonna go to bed."

"Okay." Dianna didn't even take her attention away from the news on TV.

"G'night," Clyde slurred; his eyes half closed.

I ignored him and went upstairs to my room. Turning on my phone, I opened the text from Mariah.

Hey, how's dinner?

I decided it was a little late to text back. It was only nine o'clock, but I felt worn out. Every time I hung out with Jake, it left me tired and a bit stressed. I grabbed a book from my side table and read until I fell asleep.

The next morning, I checked her phone to see if Jake had called like I'd asked him to, but I had no missed calls. I figured he'd probably gone to bed as well. It was better he hadn't called at all, instead of me missing his call. That would end with another argument.

Downstairs, Clyde was lying passed out on the couch. I guessed he had been there all night since he wore the same outfit from the night before. I knew better than to wake him when he was sleeping after a night of drinking.

I grabbed some cereal and went back upstairs to get ready for school. Usually Jake would pick me up, but who knew what his plans were that day. It wasn't that I couldn't drive, I had my license, but I didn't have a car yet.

I waited until seven before calling Jake. He picked up on the fourth ring.

"What?" he asked, without even a greeting.

"Are you bringing me to school today?"

"No," he said matter-of-factly.

"Okay then. I guess I'll call Mariah. Bye. Love you." I waited for his reply, but it never came. He hung up. I shook it off and called Mariah. Luckily, she hadn't left for school yet.

"Where's Jake?" Mariah asked while she drove.

"I don't know. Home, I guess." I stared out the window to avoid seeing Mariah's most-likely disappointed look.

"Oh, I see. Is he going to school?"

"Maybe. Why would I know?" I grew irritated with Mariah's incessant questions about Jake. Mariah sighed, giving up.

We reached the school, and I got out of the car, slamming my door shut. Clusters of freshmen gathered in the halls of the school. I shouldered my way past them and reached my locker. I spun the combination to open it and tossed my bag inside.

If Jake had come to school, he'd be in the cafeteria, so that was where I headed. As I got closer, I could hear some of Jake's friends talking. My heart swelled with anticipation. Rounding the corner into the cafeteria, disappointment flooded in as I realized Jake was not among his friends. One of them noticed me standing in the doorway and waved me over. It was Connor.

"Alana, hey," Connor said coolly. "Jake's not coming today. He's ditching with Katrina and Joe."

I cringed. Two days in a row he hung out with Katrina. Connor seemed to realize what I was thinking.

"I wouldn't worry, Katrina and Joe are together," he tried to reassure me.

The bell rang and I walked away. I didn't need anyone's pity.

Throughout the day, I texted Jake numerous times. I asked him where he was, what he was doing, whether we were hanging out that night, and would he call me or not. There were no replies.

Once the final bell rang, I needed to find a ride home. I didn't want to see Mariah again and endure her questions about Jake. Lingering on the sidewalk, I hesitated to ask Connor for a ride home, but decided maybe he could tell me more about what Jake had been up to recently.

When I walked up behind Connor, he was talking with a couple girls about a big party that weekend. I tapped his shoulder and he turned to me. Both girls, who I remembered from a party at Jake's a couple of weeks back, gave me a disgusted look. For some reason they resented me ever since I started dating Jake.

"Alana." Connor seemed surprised to see me. The girls whispered something about me behind him.

"I was wondering," I began, but one of the girls stepped forward, cutting me off.

"Connor doesn't have time to do you any favors," she grinned wickedly. Then the other girl stepped up beside her.

"Yeah, he doesn't need to waste his time on you." They laughed then placed themselves on either side of Connor and led him away. I stared at the ground, clenching my fists. When I looked up, Connor craned his neck so he could see me and mouthed, *Sorry*.

I turned away. It seemed I was stuck with Mariah as a ride home.

When I got to Mariah's car, I leaned against the passenger door, waiting. People passed by, throwing glances in my direction, but nobody stopped to talk. It seemed like an eternity had passed by the time Mariah got to her car.

"So, I'm guessing Jake's not here, considering you need me to give you a ride home. Surprise, surprise." Mariah unlocked the car and we both got in. I rolled my eyes as Mariah continued complaining. "You know, you think he could at least let you know when he isn't going to be in school. He knows that you rely on him for rides. What a jerk."

"Please, can we not talk about this? Ever?" I was exasperated by Mariah's complaints about Jake. There was no way I could listen to that the whole way home.

"Sorry, I should know by now that you will never listen to anything I have to say. Why I still even try, I don't know," Mariah said sarcastically. She started the car and drove in silence. She didn't even say goodbye when I got out of the car.

Clyde was still passed out on the couch when I went inside. It annoyed me how he could sleep away the whole day while Dianna had to work. I hated that Dianna let him walk all over her. I marched into the living room and shook Clyde's shoulder. He swung out his arm reflexively, but I dodged it and shook his shoulder again.

"Ge' off," Clyde mumbled, trying to push me away. I rolled my eyes and retreated upstairs. My phone vibrated in my jeans pocket. Whipping it out, I saw Jake's name.

"Hey! I was hoping you would call," I said cheerily. Hearing him groan, I knew he was already annoyed with me.

"You texted me like ten times today. I had to call to get you to stop," he said.

I swallowed. Of *course* that was the only reason he had called. He couldn't respond to my texts.

"Sorry. What were you doing today?" I flopped down on my bed and pushed my hair out of my face.

"I've been with some people. No one you know."

That's a lie, I thought immediately.

"Oh cool," was what I said. "Are we hanging out tonight?" I changed the subject.

"Nah, I got things to do." Someone giggled in the background. It was Katrina.

"Come on Jakey. Hang up the phone," she said.

"I gotta go, Ally." Jake hung up before I could ask who the girl was, even though I knew.

Tears swelled in my eyes. Maybe I was wrong, maybe it wasn't Katrina. But it had been her voice. Then again, Joe was there too, supposedly. I pushed away all those thoughts.

There was a knock on my door.

"Come in!" I hollered. Clyde pushed open the door and leaned against the doorframe. His eyes were bloodshot, and the scent of beer wafted through her room.

"Don't chu wake me up again. I need some sleep. An' your mum says she'll be home late." His eyes were half closed, and he swayed as he walked back down the hall.

"Thanks, Clyde," I whispered to myself. "Good man." I punched my pillow pretending it was Clyde.

My high-top sneakers sat at the end of my bed, and I pulled them on. Creeping down the stairs, I snuck out the back door so as not to wake the sleeping beauty again. The sky was darkening, and clouds were rolling in, but I decided to risk it to get out of the house.

I started down the street. I lived on a cul-de-sac with only two other houses on it, one on each side of ours. We all mostly kept to ourselves.

I paused further down the street, outside of a bright yellow house that I used to visit often, back before I started dating Jake. I knew the whole layout of the house, and even most of the small details you normally wouldn't notice. I knew there was a broken hinge on the downstairs bathroom cabinet door; I'd accidentally broken it trying to find a hiding spot for hide and seek. As far as I knew, it had never been fixed.

A shadow moved past one of the windows and I turned away quickly. What would he think, seeing me standing out there? I continued walking past the house that belonged to my ex-best friend Zac. We had been best friends since the fifth grade, up until the day I began dating Jake. We hadn't talked since then.

I had always imagined myself falling in love with Zac and being with him forever, like some grand love story. There was only one problem: when Zac professed his love for me, I realized I didn't feel the same way.

At the end of the road, I turned back toward my house. My cell phone rang. Jake's name popped up on the screen, and I debated not answering but didn't want to risk angering him again.

"Hey," I said.

"Where are you?"

"Walking down my street, why?" I asked.

"I'm at your house, so hurry up." He hung up. I hadn't seen him drive by, which meant he had been at someone's house who lived on my street. Joe lived somewhere nearby, so he must have been there. I breathed a sigh of relief. If he had been at Joe's, that meant he hadn't been alone with Katrina.

When I reached Zac's house again, he was at his mailbox. I prayed he wouldn't notice me, but he did. He smiled at me.

"Hey, Ally," he said. I smiled back, hoping he wouldn't notice the pain it caused me to talk to him. "Long time, no see."

"Yeah. I've been busy," I lied. I'd hardly done anything all week.

"Me too." He rested his arm on his mailbox. "So, how have you been?" he asked casually.

"Fine," I said, hoping to end the conversation.

"That's good. How's Jake?" he asked.

"Fine," I repeated.

"That's good."

This conversation was going in circles.

"I have to go. Sorry, it was nice talking to you." I turned away before he could say anything else.

Jake sat in his truck in my driveway. He saw me coming in his rearview mirror and hopped out of his truck.

"What took you so long?" he asked.

I knew he'd seen me talking with Zac, so I didn't try to hide it.

"Zac stopped me to talk. I haven't talked to him in over a year." I wanted to make sure Jake knew I wasn't talking to Zac on a regular basis. Jake knew how close I'd been to Zac before, and that Zac had loved me, so he didn't particularly care for him.

"That's nice of him to want to talk to you." Jake worded it almost as if it were an insult. "I mean, he probably has more important things to do."

I gulped back the lump in my throat. "I'm sure he does." My voice wavered. "What are you doing here?"

"I thought you wanted to hangout," he said. I *had* wanted to hangout, but now I wasn't so sure. "I can leave if you want."

"No, that's okay. Let's go inside."

Jake followed me inside to the kitchen.

"Want some food?" I asked Jake, who stood in the doorway staring into the living room at Clyde who lay sprawled on the couch.

"Sure." He sauntered over to the counter where I stood and wrapped his arms around my waist. "Doesn't Clyde have a job or something?"

I leaned back against his chest. "He claims to have one, but every time I'm home, he's passed out on the couch, or at the bar." I shrugged. "What do you want to eat?" I opened one of the cabinets.

"I guess I'll have one of those." He pointed to the box of chocolate chip granola bars. I grabbed two from the box and put one into Jake's hand, which was still around my waist. He turned me around and I put my arms around his neck.

"I don't like you being home alone with Clyde when he's drinking," Jake said quietly, so as not to be overheard if Clyde woke up. I smiled. He *did* still care about me.

"He's pretty harmless, as long as I don't wake him up," I said. It was true; Clyde had never hurt me or Dianna. Not even when he was drinking, but he was a jerk.

"Still, I don't want to take any chances. You should call me whenever you're home alone with him and I'll come over or pick you up. It would make me feel better." Jake looked away from me. It amazed me how he could go from insulting me one minute, to being overprotective of me the next.

"That's really not necessary." I pulled away from him. "Come on; let's go up to my room." I led Jake up to my room and shut the door behind me. I sat at my desk, the rolling chair making the whooshing sound it always made when I sat down. Jake sat across from me on my bed. He laid down and propped his head up on his fist so he could look at me.

"Whatcha wanna do?" he asked, grinning. I twirled around in my chair. Jake hardly ever smiled at me like that anymore, it gave me butterflies. His phone beeped and I stopped spinning.

"Who is it?" I asked.

"None of your business." Jake got up off the bed and walked to the door. "I'll call you later," he said without looking back.

I let out a puff of air. Happy moment gone.

"Yeah, sure," I whispered.

A couple seconds later, the front door slammed shut. I turned in my chair and glanced at the picture that hung behind my desk. It was taken a few years ago at a camp my grandparents owned. Zac had been a regular at the camp; I brought him almost every time we went. I'd been too lazy to replace it after we'd stopped being friends.

I hadn't seen my grandmother in a few weeks, even though she only lived five minutes away. So many things had happened since that picture was taken. I probably wasn't the same girl my grandmother remembered, which was why I went over there less and less.

My phone vibrated in my pocket. I hoped it was Jake explaining why he left so suddenly. My hopes were dashed when Mariah's name flashed across the screen followed by her text, *hey, sorry about earlier. Wanna hangout?*

I smiled, relieved that Mariah was no longer upset with me. I typed back to Mariah. *Sure! My house?* A few seconds later came the reply, *be there in 5.*

The next morning, I woke up to the sun's rays streaming through my window. I swatted at the alarm clock on my bedside table and thought about what Mariah had told me the day before. I'd been open with her and told her about how Jake was hanging out with Katrina, and I suspected he might be cheating. Mariah, trying to keep her harsh feelings against Jake at bay, simply suggested I make Jake feel like he was losing me. That way, he would be more likely to stay away from Katrina and hopefully put more of his focus back on our relationship.

I didn't like the idea, knowing how upset Jake got when I didn't answer his calls or texts, but decided it was worth a shot to get him to return his attention to me. I started with his text waiting for me on my phone in the morning.

Do you need a ride to school? It read. I would normally reply 'yes' in a heartbeat, but today, I wrote *nope, Mariah's bringing me.* I received no reply and knew I had already ticked him off.

Mariah picked me up and when we got to school, she asked, "Any contact from Jake yet?"

"Not since he asked if I needed a ride this morning." I was becoming more and more unsure of this plan.

"Don't worry; I'm sure everything will be fine. He hardly ever talks to you even when he's not mad at you." Mariah's eyes widened as she realized she'd said the wrong thing.

I snapped. "What do you know about how much Jake talks to me? You never even bother to stand near us when I'm with him. I have to get to class." I got out of Mariah's car and slammed the door shut. Mariah hopped out after me.

"You know what? I'm sick of this! I try to help you because you think Jake is cheating on you, which believe me, is probably a ninety-nine percent chance of being true, and all you do is get mad when I say one wrong thing! I'm done trying to help you. I should have never texted you yesterday. Don't bother waiting by my car today. Find someone else to bring you home." Mariah finished with a flourish of her arms and stormed off into the school.

I stood slack-jawed, thinking about everything Mariah said and decided it wasn't *my* fault she didn't like Jake. She could at least *try* to get along with him occasionally.

Of course, at the end of the day, I was without a ride. I stood on the sidewalk, feeling much like I had the day before, pretending to be waiting for someone as I debated who to ask. I could always call Clyde, but who knew if he was sober enough to drive. Jake was out of the question; he hadn't spoken with me all day. Besides, I didn't see his truck in the parking lot. I could always walk home.

"Hey Alana." I turned to find Connor standing beside me. "Jake told me you're mad at him or something?"

"He did?" I was surprised Jake even mentioned me to any of his friends.

"Well, kind of. He said he wouldn't be bringing anyone home today, including you, because he said you didn't want to ride with him," Connor explained. "I read between the lines."

"Not exactly. I mean, I never said I didn't want to ride with him; I already had a ride. This morning, that is." I glanced around, indicating there was no one waiting to take me home.

"You need a ride?" Connor offered.

"Yeah, I do." I hated to impose on anyone, but regrettably, I often had to because of my lack of a car and unwillingness to walk or take the bus.

"That's fine. I've got nowhere to be today," he smiled. "Anything for Jake's girl." He nudged my arm playfully and I finally smiled back.

Chapter Three
Zac

Dad had been right and there was nothing to find in the woods behind the park.

Maybe she's still out there. Maybe she's still alive, part of me hoped, even though they'd found blood in the woods where we happened to have been the night before.

I dreamt of her that night and when I woke, I half expected her to be there with me as if we'd never left the house that night.

But she wasn't. She was still gone. And I was going to find her.

Rolling out of bed, I grabbed my phone from the side table and headed to the kitchen to make a strong cup of coffee. I'd never cared much for coffee before, but I figured if I was going to start drinking it, today would be the day.

I munched on a granola bar as I searched my phone for anything that might help me figure out what happened that night. There were no recent pictures on my phone, and I'd made no posts on any social media. But I wasn't the only one there that night.

As soon as I clicked onto Ally's Facebook page, I knew I'd made a mistake. Post after post of people sharing their worries and theories on where she'd wound up. I almost threw my phone across the room.

Half the people posting on her page had probably never spoken to her. My hand shook as I set my phone down, locking it so the posts would disappear.

I closed my eyes and a gunshot reverberated through my head as if it were next to me. Slamming my hands on the counter, I jumped up. My breathing was ragged, and I whipped around as if there to be someone else in my kitchen with me, but there wasn't. The shot had been in my mind. *A memory,* something told me.

"Hey Zac," Dad greeted me as he came into the kitchen. "The police want to talk to you again." He gave me an apologetic look, but I knew there was nothing he could do to get me out of this.

A police car waited in the driveway. The same two officers who had questioned me in the hospital got out of the car and greeted us as Dad and I stepped out onto the porch. They read me my Miranda rights and informed me that I was a suspect in Ally's disappearance and had to answer some questions down at the station. I could either wait for my parents to find me an attorney to be present with me during the interrogation, or I would be provided with one.

Apparently, my parents had already hired an attorney, which didn't give me much confidence in them believing I was innocent.

Maybe you aren't, an intrusive thought popped up at the back of my mind. Fear clutched me and I held my breath, waiting for the thought to fade back into oblivion. But it didn't.

"Can't they leave me alone for one day?" I said, trying to distract myself.

"Our attorney, Bonnie will meet us at the station," Mom said, holding her phone in her hand as if she'd just spoken with her.

On the car ride to the station, Mom couldn't let me sit in our silence. Instead, she brought up the last thing I wanted to talk about.

"The doctor gave us a referral for a therapist," she said.

"I don't need therapy," I snapped.

"It's to help you deal with the loss of Ally and possibly help you recover your memories," she explained. It was the same explanation the doctor had given.

"What if I don't want to remember?" I murmured. *What if I hurt her?*

Mom sighed. "If I believed that, I'd let it go. Go one time and if you hate it, you can stop going."

"Fine, whatever," I agreed, thinking the conversation would be forgotten anyway and I'd never actually have to go to therapy.

The silence returned and changed to a high-pitched ringing as I stared out the window, not truly seeing anything.

At the police station, the officers waited in the interrogation room. Bonnie met us at the door, running through a quick overview of what I could expect.

"Don't answer anything unless I give you the okay," she said, flicking her sleek ponytail over her shoulder. "And if you don't know an answer, don't say anything."

I nodded like a bobblehead, not truly present. I'd hardly heard a word she'd said.

"Good afternoon, Zac," one of the police officers greeted me as we walked into the interrogation room.

"Good afternoon," I replied.

"Have a seat." The police officer gestured to the chair across from himself. I sat down in the chair, and Bonnie sat next to me. With her fancy pinstriped, gray suit, she was how I'd always pictured a lawyer, very put together and serious.

"My name is Detective Johnson, and this is Officer Monroe." Detective Johnson held a hand over his heart as he introduced himself and the other man at the table. It explained why Detective Johnson wasn't wearing a uniform like Officer Monroe.

Detective Johnson pressed the start button on the recorder in the middle of the table.

"Please state your name for the record," he said.

"Zachary Martin." My voice wavered, and my mind raced with all the questions that they might ask. The officer stated a few more things for the record, like the date and time, but the roaring in my ears had come back and it was hard for me to focus. Taking a deep breath, I closed my eyes as the officer spoke again.

"We need some details about what happened at the park on the night of October thirteenth." Detective Johnson studied me with his dark brown, almost black, eyes.

Sweat beaded on my upper lip and my leg bounced beneath the table. I cleared my throat, but before I could say anything, Bonnie said, "My client has been diagnosed with traumatic amnesia and had no memory of the night of the thirteenth."

"We've been informed of that. If you may, Zac, start from the beginning of the night up until you can no longer remember," Detective Johnson prompted.

So, I relayed what I remembered, starting with playing Uno in my bedroom, and ending with Ally running to the park and greeting Mariah.

"Do you recall anyone else at the park that night?" Officer Monroe asked.

Bonnie nodded at me when I looked at her for the okay to speak.

"There was a bunch of kids from our school, but that's all I remember."

Officer Monroe whispered something to Detective Johnson.

"Now, you're positive you're telling us everything you know?" Detective Johnson asked, his gaze piercing.

"Yes."

Detective Johnson jotted something down in a notepad he pulled out from his jacket pocket. "And you have no idea if Alana was having trouble with anyone, or had made any enemies lately?"

"No. I can't think of anyone who would want to hurt her." I shook my head. "I thought she hadn't been found-" My words stuck in my throat, and I couldn't get them out.

Officer Monroe shook his head. "She's considered a missing person, but with the amount of blood found at the scene, I don't want you to get your hopes up."

"So, the blood you found, it was hers?" Breathing was becoming harder.

"The blood we found matches her blood type."

My mind whirled. "So, it could be someone else." I didn't even believe the words. Deep down, I knew the truth, I *felt* it.

"We'd like to speak to your mother to make sure the timing of things is how you remember them," Detective Johnson said. "If you can think of anything else from that night-" he handed me a card with his name and number on it - "don't hesitate to give me a call."

Officer Monroe walked me out of the room, while Bonnie remained to sit in on the conversation with Mom.

"Thank you for joining us Mrs. Martin," Detective Johnson asked after Mom had gone in. "Do you recall Alana and Zac returning to the house at any point in time the night of the incident?"

"Oh, please call me Carrie," she responded, and then the door was shut, and I couldn't hear them anymore. I sat on a bench beside Dad.

The police station wasn't very busy, but there was enough noise that it was overwhelming. It reminded me of an office, and I couldn't reconcile the normalcy of the atmosphere with the horrific event I was supposed to be trying to remember.

"I think I need to step outside," I said, not waiting to see if Dad would respond before I ran out of the station. I could hardly breathe, like in the hospital, it had felt as if the walls had been closing in on me.

The chilly, fall air seared my lungs, but it reminded me that this was real. My heart pounded and the hair on my arms and back of my neck stood up.

Even after hearing Officer Monroe say there was little chance Ally had survived, I held onto an unrealistic notion she was alive and well, and all of this was some big misunderstanding. She'd be found alive in a few hours, or days, and all would go back to normal.

Dad came to sit on the sidewalk beside me, grunting from the effort of getting down so low.

"I know what the officer's said, but don't give up hope yet," he said, putting his arm around me.

They let us go home after they finished talking with Mom, and I was able to change back into comfy clothes.

Both of my parents had to leave for work as soon as we made it home, leaving me home alone, but I couldn't shake the feeling of being watched.

"I need to get out of this house," I mumbled to myself.

I didn't bother changing out of my sweatpants and shoved my feet into my work boots, leaving them untied as I walked out the door.

The crisp fall air hit me and sent a shiver through me, but I didn't turn back for a jacket. The cold would keep me focused. Maybe.

Ally's colder. I shook my head, trying to clear away that thought.

The streets were littered with dead leaves, and they crunched under my boots as I walked toward the park. I figured I'd have better luck finding clues in the daytime. I couldn't imagine the police would have missed anything, but I had nothing better to do and I wouldn't sit idly by while Ally was still missing.

Her body is missing. Ally is dead. That stupid voice said. I almost wanted to argue with it, but then I think that would make me crazy.

I'm not crazy, I thought.

Shoving a hand through my hair I huffed a breath and ducked under the *crime scene* tape blocking off the park. No one was around and I figured they hadn't come to clean up the tape yet.

To my left was the see-saw, and I doubted Ally had gone anywhere near that. But straight ahead was the tall wooden tower we often hung out at the top of, and behind that the swings. Two places we spent way too much time when we were younger, thinking we were so cool.

I went to the tower first. Apparently, this is where I'd been found, unconscious at the bottom. I thought seeing it might spark some kind of memory, but I still remembered nothing after our arrival at the park that night.

Climbing to the top of the tower, I scraped my hand on the wood and cursed. I'd been avoiding using my injured arm and wound up hurting myself anyway.

The tower had been built years ago and never been maintained, so the wood was splintering in many places and should probably be torn down. The base platform always creaked whenever I stepped on it, and when I was up top, I swore the whole thing was swaying.

But I always risked it anyway, and I did so again that day. You could see the whole park from up there, and it was the perfect vantage point to try and figure out where Ally might have spent her time the night she disappeared.

I stared down at the base of the tower, thinking about what would happen if the whole thing decided to collapse. A glint caught my eye as I moved to the right. It disappeared, but when I moved back to the left, I caught it again.

Hopping from platform to platform, I descended the tower and headed for the spot where I'd seen the glint. At first, there was no sign of what I'd seen, but as I kicked the woodchips around, I saw it. A phone.

Ally's phone.

I picked it up and traced the small crack across the screen. Of course, it was dead, so it didn't turn on when I tried. Slipping it into my pocket, I headed for home. I'd charge her phone and see if she had anything on there that would help me remember what happened.

My heart was racing so fast, I worried I might actually pass out, so I sat for a few seconds with my head between my knees on the base platform of the tower.

"This could help me find her," I said. "This could solve everything. Or... It could help nothing. There might be nothing on it." I needed to reality check myself. I didn't want to get my hopes up and then have that crushing weight of disappointment shove me back into a spiral.

"Zac?" A familiar voice came from the sidewalk behind me. I lifted my head and turned to see Mariah, Ally's best friend, walking across the woodchips toward me.

"Mariah? What are you doing here?" I asked, shoving my hand into my pocket and gripping Ally's phone as if she might try to take it away from me even though there was no way she even knew I had it.

"I was about to ask you the same thing," she said, raising her brows.

"I was hoping I'd be able to jog my memory by coming out here," I explained, leaving out the fact that I'd found the phone. "But no luck."

She rocked on her heels, blowing out a long breath.

"It's so crazy what happened," she said. "I can't believe she's really gone."

I cocked my head to the side. "She's still missing, so there's a chance she's alive, right?"

Mariah's eyes widened and then she shook her head. "Yeah, I guess. The police said something about the amount of blood they found and the chances of her making it being slim, but crazier things have happened." Tears glistened in her eyes, and she wiped them away. "Sorry," she murmured. "I don't mean to be so negative. I miss her so much."

"Don't be. She was your best friend, I expected you to be upset." I stood but kept my hands in my pockets. "I miss her, too."

Mariah bit her trembling lip. "I should be getting home."

"Were you there that night?" I asked, hoping she might be able to help me recover some memories.

"Um, yeah. I was," she said. "But I left before it happened." Her phone rang and she held it up. "Sorry, it's my mom. I'll see you at school." She answered her phone as she walked away. I followed her out of the park and then we went in opposite directions.

At home, I plugged in Ally's phone and waited for it to light up. Once it powered on, I went to the photos. The last one taken was of us on top of the tower. It was surreal to see the picture but not remember it being taken.

I sat on the floor with my back leaning against my bed and I let my head fall back as I stared at the ceiling.

"*Ally, don't go back down there.*" I stood with my arms propped on the railing of the tower, my back to Ally, but I craned my neck so I could see her.

She put her hand on her hip. "Give me a reason to stay up here."

Mariah had already jumped down to the next platform.

"One reason: your best friend, a.k.a. me, is up here, and..." I hesitated, unsure if I should say the next words or not. There was a time when I'd loved Ally, and told her so, but now, after being rejected by her and going years without speaking, it didn't feel the same. Thinking about saying those words again seemed wrong, and they stuck in my throat. *"And it's supposed to be our night,"* I said instead, closing my eyes and turning toward the front of the tower.

"I know, I know. But we need to live a little, have some fun. Come on, Zac, everyone else is down there." She pointed to them all below the tower. *"I'll come back up later. Or you could come down with us."* She grinned.

"No thank you." I stood and rested my chin on the railing, staring out into the darkness.

I blinked and was back in the present. Gasping, I gulped down breaths, assuming I had stopped breathing while I'd had that flashback.

"What the hell?" I gripped Ally's phone so tight, it kept taking screenshots from all the buttons being pressed at the same time. I dropped it and covered my face with my hands.

The doorbell rang, making me jump out of my skin.

Josh waited outside when I opened the door, and a sense of relief washed over me seeing him. He was my best friend, besides Ally, and it was nice to see someone other than my parents who I could vent to.

"Hey, man," Josh greeted me, giving me a sad smile. "I heard what happened and I figured you might want someone to talk to."

For the first time in our friendship, I hugged him. I think it surprised him as much as me, but he didn't say anything, just hugged me back.

"It's so crazy," I choked out, managing to hold back my tears. Pulling away from him, I laughed as he straightened his flat-brimmed hat that I'd knocked off kilter.

"I know. I couldn't believe it when I heard. Or saw, I guess. It's all over Facebook." He rubbed the back of his neck. "And I can't believe you were there for it."

I sucked in a breath through my teeth. "Well, I don't remember it. All I remember is walking to the park with Ally, and then nothing. I don't even know who else was there other than Mariah."

Josh's brow furrowed. "Mariah was there?"

"Yeah. I vaguely remember seeing her that night."

"So, you do remember something then?" He cocked his head to the side.

I waved my hand through the air. "Nah, man. I've got nothing. But mom wants me to go to therapy, so I'll let you know how that goes."

We both laughed. It wasn't something either of us would have ever considered before. *Therapy.* It almost seemed like a taboo word around here. But the more I thought about it, the more it seemed like it might actually help.

I shook my head. I didn't need help from anyone but my family and friends. I could get through this without some doctor trying to tell me how to breathe or how to feel feelings.

"If you ever need to talk about it, or anything, let me know. I know we don't usually talk about stuff like this, but I'm here if you need me," Josh said. "I'm sorry about Ally, and I hope they find her body soon so this can all be over."

Body. Josh didn't believe she was alive either. The knife in my gut twisted slightly. It was waiting for the moment when I lost all hope that Ally was alive to slice me open, but I wouldn't give up. Not until I found her. Despite the fact that every rational part of me was screaming that she was dead and gone.

"I will," I told Josh. "Thanks for stopping by."

He initiated the hug that time, and I held on tight before letting him go. I wasn't normally a hugging person, but it seemed to heal something in me, or maybe it tricked me into thinking that I was holding myself together.

Back in my room, I picked up Ally's phone from the floor. I studied the picture of her for a few seconds, trying to memorize the light freckles across her nose, in case I never saw them again. Shaking my head, I scrolled to the next picture. It was blurry and crooked as if it had been taken accidentally. I couldn't make out anything or anyone.

This is useless. I scrolled to the next picture, and it was another blurry random photo. This time, Jake's face stood out amidst the rest of the random blurred faces.

"So, he *was* there." There were no more pictures of that night, and I didn't want to totally invade Ally's privacy.

Not that it matters since she's dead. No. *She's not dead,* I tried to combat my doubts.

I took a deep breath. This phone was probably considered evidence and would need to go to the police, but I wasn't ready to deal with that.

"How could this happen?" I spotted something out of the corner of my eye under my bed. Ally's bag she had brought to my house that night. I pulled it out.

Footsteps on the stairs told me that Mom was home from work. She walked to my doorway and leaned against the doorframe, knocking on the door with a grin.

"Knock, knock," she said.

"Come in," I sighed.

Her smile turned down as she noticed the bag in my lap. "She brought this here that night," I explained to. She came in and knelt by my side.

"We should return this to her mother." She gave me a sorrowful look that almost made me want to scream. I couldn't take the pitying looks and I hadn't even gotten the worst of it yet. When I went back to school, I could only imagine how bad it would be.

"Yeah," I whispered, gripping the strap of the duffle bag tight in my fist. "We should."

While we were out, I told Mom about the phone, and we dropped it off at the police station. They had a million questions about how I'd found it, and I told them exactly what happened, but I couldn't help but think they suspected me of lying. There was nothing I could do about that, though. They also refused to tell me if they'd learned anything that might help find Ally, so I figured I was on my own with my investigation.

We stopped at Ally's grandmother's house next, where Dianna was staying. I assumed it was too difficult to be in her own house without Ally.

Dianna invited us inside, and Ally's grandmother poured tea for us all. It was strange to see Dianna after all the years of her practically ignoring Ally. I almost wanted to ask her if she really cared that her daughter was missing, but of course, I would never.

"Thank you so much for bringing this back to me," Dianna said, setting Ally's bag to the side. "It's been-" Tears welled in her eyes and a choked sob broke free from her.

Mom reached over and placed her hand on Dianna's knee. "We're here to help in any way you need."

"Thank you," Dianna gasped. "And thank you for noticing that Ally was missing. I wouldn't have, since I thought she was at your house."

I perked up. This was new information for me. Mom hadn't told me *she'd* been the one to alert everyone that Ally was missing.

"As soon as we got the call about Zac, I started asking around about Ally. I knew she should have been with him," Mom explained. "And I knew that I'd want someone to do the same, if the situation was reversed."

Dianna nodded. Tears streamed down her cheeks. "I'm so sorry," she said, wiping her eyes.

"Don't be." Mom patted her knee again and leaned back. "You have every right to be upset."

"You're going to think I'm being morbid, or crazy," she sighed, and shook her head. Ally's grandmother stood and left the room.

"I have this feeling, and I hate it, but it's like I *know* Ally's not out there anymore. I can't feel her like I used to. Like I said, crazy."

"Not at all," Mom said.

"Of course I hope she's still out there, I don't know what I'll do if she's not." She broke down into a fit of sobs. We ended up having to leave.

I was at a loss for words after hearing Dianna's thoughts. If Ally's own mother believed she was dead, then why should I keep believing she wasn't?

"I set up a therapy session for you for tomorrow after school," Mom said, interrupting my spiraling, as she drove. "I figured the sooner the better."

I didn't argue, even though I had no desire to attend the appointment. I'd do it, but I wasn't making any promises that I'd stick with it.

"And your dad's going to be gone for the next couple of weeks for work, so if you need anything, come to me, okay?" I could hear the worry in her voice. It was almost palpable in the car, like she thought I might breakdown at any second.

"Okay," I said. I could hold myself together, with or without therapy.

I stared out the window at the passing houses and wondered which of them had experienced a tragedy like this. Or if they all had perfect, uneventful lives.

"Were there any pictures on Ally's phone of the two of you?" Mom asked. We'd pulled into the driveway, and she put the car into park, turning to look at me.

"Uh, yeah." I wasn't sure why she was asking.

"Did you send it to yourself so that you could have it?"

I slowly shook my head. That would have been a good idea. I should have sent myself the picture of Jake too, then I could approach him about it. I didn't have the proof, in case he denied being there.

It wasn't that I really thought Jake had done anything to hurt her, he didn't seem like that kind of guy, but his relationship with Ally had been far from perfect. And that was from what I saw from afar. Ally and I hadn't talked while she'd been with Jake, but you'd have to be blind to not see how unhappy they were.

They'd broken up a few days before she died, which was the only reason Ally was hanging out with me that night. While they were together, she refused to even look at me most days. I'd accepted it, and moved on, but then she came crashing back into my life.

"Zac?" Mom tapped my knee. "You coming inside?"

I'd zoned out. Blinking rapidly to refocus, I got out of the car and followed Mom inside. She started dinner while I headed upstairs to lie down for a while.

I closed my eyes, thinking of where I'd last seen Ally, on the swings. It was easy to remember a time when we'd both been oblivious to the rest of the world and truly happy. Before she ever started dating Jake.

"What is that?" Ally snorted, laughing at the book I held. "I can't believe you brought your homework." She moved her swing toward mine and grabbed the book from my hands, tossing it to the side.

"Hey! I am about to fail this class; I need to do this extra credit." I couldn't help but smile despite my book lying in the dirt.

"Don't you love it here? I love it here." She gazed up into the sky, twisting her swing this way and that. Butterflies churned my stomach as I watched her.

"I love being here with you," I said, working up to telling her how I really felt about her. She closed her eyes and smiled. Then her phone rang. She groaned as she read at the name scrawled across the screen.

"What?" she answered it. There was a long pause, and then she said, "fine, yeah. I'm on my way." She gave me an apologetic look as she hung up her phone. "Sorry..." she muttered. "My mom wants me to come home for dinner. I don't know why she cares today. She's so random."

"It's fine. I have to get this extra credit done anyways." I stood from the swing and picked up my book, shoving it into my bag.

"I can help you with your extra credit. I'm acing English," she offered with a smile. "C'mon."

We headed back to her house, and I decided I would tell her I loved her another day. It could wait.

I opened my eyes as Mom called me down for dinner. I'd thought Ally had been so happy, but I remembered how miserable she seemed that night we'd gone back to her house. Clyde had been there, passed out on the couch. Her mother was trying her best to be a good host, but I could see the bags under her eyes and hear the exhaustion in her voice. Maybe Ally's life hadn't been all that great *before* Jake either.

Chapter Four
Alana
Eleven days before

Connor and I were halfway to my house when Jake called.

"Hey, Jake." I tried not to sound too eager to talk to him, sticking to Mariah's plan.

"Hey, Alana. Where are you?" I could hear the tension in his voice.

"Connor's giving me a ride home." *I should have lied,* was my immediate thought after the words came out of my mouth. I scrunched my nose and braced for the outburst.

"What? Why the hell are you with Connor? Why didn't you call me?" Jake flipped.

I shut my eyes tight. It was an automatic reaction to his yelling.

"He offered, and you had already left," I said through gritted teeth. We pulled up to the curb near my house. "Look, I needed a ride, and Connor was nice enough to give me one. Call me later when you aren't in such a bad mood." I hung up and shoved my phone into the side pocket of my backpack.

"Thank you for the ride," I said quietly, looking down at my hands. "I'm really sorry, I think Jake-"

"Don't be. Jake's going to be mad no matter who gives you a ride home. He'll get over it." Connor waved it off.

"I'm not so sure, but we'll go with that." I smiled despite the feeling of unease at how Jake would react to me hanging up on him. "I should get inside." I climbed out of the truck and turned back to say goodbye.

"If anything happens," Connor paused and seemed to change his mind. "Be careful."

Inside, Clyde stood in the kitchen, surprisingly sober, making a sandwich.

"Who was that boy who dropped you off?" Clyde asked when I walked into the kitchen.

"A friend. Why do you care?" I was irritated that Clyde was there, again, at my house, while Dianna was at work making money to buy the food that he was eating. And he had clearly been watching me through the window.

"Hey, I care. I care that you were with someone other than your boyfriend, who stopped by here earlier asking for you." Clyde waved the knife around that he had been spreading his peanut butter with.

"You're lying. Jake wasn't here." He liked to taunt me. Once he had even told me that Jake had asked him for permission to marry me. I knew well enough to never trust Clyde.

"Fine. Don't believe me." Clyde licked the peanut butter from the knife and tossed it onto the counter.

"Fine. I won't." I took the stairs two at a time. I couldn't get away from Clyde fast enough. He repulsed me. I slammed my bedroom door shut and locked it for good measure.

Expecting a couple angry phone calls from Jake by then, I checked my pockets for my phone and realized it must have fallen out of my bag in Connor's truck. I threw myself on my bed in frustration. I probably *had* gotten calls from Jake, and the more calls I missed, the more irate he would become. There was no way I could contact Connor to let him know he had my phone either, because I didn't know his number.

I would have to go to Jake's house and pray he was there so I could talk to him and explain everything. Of course, I would have to take Clyde's car, and he was not exactly one to let others drive his baby, even though it was an old beat-up station wagon.

I trudged back downstairs to find Clyde eating his sandwich on the couch. I grudgingly sat on the couch as well, as far from him as possible.

"So, Jake was here earlier?" I began.

Clyde glanced over at me, chewing with his mouth open. I cringed.

"You believe me now?" he asked, spitting as he spoke. I nodded. "He stopped by before you got home, said something about you ignoring him, and then told me to let you know he was here."

I sighed. Of course that's why he had been here. Not because he was worried, but because I had the nerve to ignore him. I changed my mind. I wasn't going to go see him. He could call my phone all he wanted, and at least I didn't have to hear it ringing incessantly.

I jumped as the phone in the kitchen rang. My heartbeat quickened. *Does Jake know my home number?*

"Get that, would you?" Clyde waved his hand toward the phone.

Grumbling, I got up to answer the phone. It wasn't like he should be answering our phone anyway.

"Hello?" I answered it hesitantly, hoping not to hear Jake's voice on the other end. A moment passed when there was no answer, and finally there was an intake of breath.

"Dianna?"

I slammed the phone back down. Unable to move for a full minute, I stood there with my hand gripping the phone, not comprehending how this could happen.

There's no way. I must be crazy.

But there was no mistaking that voice. It sang me to sleep every night for nearly seven years, until I claimed I was too old to be tucked in by my daddy anymore. That was the same year he'd left. He hadn't once contacted us... Until now.

I ran upstairs, tears streaming down my face as I buried my head in my pillow. I already had too much going on. Why did he choose now to try to reach out to us?

The phone rang again, and at first, I chose not to answer but realized it would be much worse if Clyde answered.

"Stop," was the first thing I said. "Please, stop calling." My sobbing became audible, and I hung up the phone again. The worst part was my dad thought that I was Dianna. He called me Dianna. That hammered home how long it had been since he had left.

I needed to get outside. The walls were beginning to close in around me. Pulling myself together as I walked past Clyde on the couch, I walked down to the end of my driveway and sat on the sidewalk and rested my head on my knees. I thought back to the last time I'd heard that voice.

"Please, Danny. Please leave before you wake up Ally. I can't do this anymore; I can't pretend I still love you," Dianna spoke softly. My door was cracked open, and my parents' voices drifted in. I slid out of bed and crawled over to the door. I watched as my dad tried to persuade my mom to let him stay.

"I'll do anything. Let me make it up to you." Danny reached out for Dianna's hand, but she pulled away.

"I can never forgive you. I would rather forget you. Please, leave, now." Tears rolled down Dianna's face. I'd never seen my mom cry before.

"Okay." Danny gave up. I saw the light leave his eyes and I forgot that I was supposed to be asleep. I pushed slightly on the door.
"Daddy." I stood and ran to him. Dianna caught me and held me in her arms until Danny was gone.

I blamed Dianna for my dad leaving for a long time. That was the reason that Dianna was so distant with me. It was hard knowing that I'd hurt her by blaming her for so long. By the time I'd learned that my dad had cheated on Dianna, we had already fallen into a rhythm of icing each other out, and I had no idea how to break out of that.

Picking my head up, I noticed a friend of Zac's, Aaron, pulling into Zac's driveway and I scowled.

Before I knew it, I stood at the end of Zac's driveway. Aaron and Zac had already gone inside, not noticing my approach. I made my way up the short patch of pavement but stopped short.

What am I doing? I had no right to be there. Turning on my heel, I made my way back to the road. My whole body shook and I nearly fainted when I saw Jake speeding down the street toward me. Stumbling backwards, I tripped and fell onto the sidewalk. I tried to push myself back to my feet, but all my strength had left.

"Alana!" Jake bellowed as he jumped out of his truck and came trudging toward me.

"W-what?" I cowered on the sidewalk. Jake held his phone out in front of me.

"I've called and texted you at least five times!"

Five times? That's it? I thought.

He continued, "You hung up on me! Why?"

"Jake, I-I'm sorry. I left my phone in Connor's truck." That set him off.

"You should never have been with Connor in the first place!" Jake put his hands on his head. "Never mind. We're done. I'm done. I deserve better."

I snapped.

"You deserve better? Jake." I laughed. "I have done absolutely nothing wrong." I stood and took a step toward him. "I call you at least twice a day, even when I know you won't answer, because you get pissed if I don't call. Of course, you get pissed when I do call, too. I'm always available to hang out with you, even when I'm not *really* available. If you tell me it's none of my business, I stay out of it. I don't fight back, I don't act jealous, and I do everything you tell me to do," I spat. "If anyone deserves better, it's me!" I stormed off toward my house.

"Wait! Alana, come back," he called after me.

I kept walking, trying not to look back. I nearly made it to my driveway when I stopped. Turning back to Jake, I was surprised to see him still standing in the same spot I'd left him, looking vulnerable.

"Ally, please," he said, his voice almost inaudible from that distance. The thought of going into my house where Clyde was most likely passed out on the couch, and the phone might ring with my dad on the other end, made me stop. Jake was all I had.

My resolve crumbled and I caved. Smiling weakly, I made my way back to him.

"I'm sorry," I murmured. He pulled me close and I wrapped my arms around him.

"Let's forget about it. I gotta go, but I'll call you later." Jake kissed me softly and left.

I sank onto the sidewalk and realized what I'd done. Once again, I'd failed at trying to let Jake go. After everything he had put me through, I still loved him. I would do anything for him.

Zac stood at his window, and he quickly pulled away when he saw me looking.

The next day, Connor gave me back my phone and everything went back to normal. Jake was ignoring my texts, and Mariah was still upset and not talking to me. We had been in many fights before, though, and Mariah always forgave me, or vice versa. It was only a matter of time. I'd almost completely forgotten my dad had called, never bothering to tell Dianna. Hopefully, he would listen and never call again. However, when I got home from school and saw Clyde's face, I knew that had not been the case.

Clyde was furious. He had always been touchy about the subject of my dad, worrying that deep down Dianna still loved him. Clyde and I both knew that if Dianna ever left him, he would have nothing. He had no money of his own and no family to rely on.

"Why is he even calling?" Clyde asked.

I shrugged; I really had no idea. It wasn't like I'd talked to him at all.

Nevertheless, Clyde gave me an accusing look. "You told him to call, didn't you? You want him to come back so that I'll have to leave."

"I would never! He left us. I don't want him to come back, ever," I defended myself, omitting the truth that I'd love for Clyde to leave.

"Yeah, sure. Well, your mom shouldn't have to deal with this. No one will tell her, right?"

I knew Clyde would do everything in his power to keep my dad out of our lives.

"She won't be too happy if she finds out you've been keeping this from her. It would probably be safer to tell her." I knew this was the truth, but I also knew that Clyde would never let her find out if he could help it.

"Shut up. I'm thinking," Clyde snapped.

I left the kitchen and went up to my room. In a way, I hoped Dianna would find out Danny was calling, then maybe they'd get back together, and Clyde would be gone from our lives forever. That would never happen, though, and I wasn't sure I even wanted that to happen.

I plopped onto my bed and closed my eyes, imagining a life where my dad had stayed. There was nothing. My mind came up blank. What would life be like if my dad had stuck around, and fought for Dianna? Would it have changed anything? Or were my parents doomed not to be together? Pushing aside those thoughts I tried calling Jake. No answer, of course, and I fell asleep waiting for him to call back.

That night, Dianna came home late, again. It was yet another 'make your own dinner' night. I couldn't help but feel like maybe I was better off not telling Dianna about the calls. After all, my dad was the reason that my relationship with Dianna was not so warm and fuzzy.

Before I fell asleep that night, my phone vibrated on my side table. Groaning, I rolled over and hit the green button without checking to see who it was.

"Hello?" I yawned.

"Hey babe." Jake's voice instantly made me more alert.

"What's up?" I asked, wondering why he was calling so late. It was nearly midnight.

"Don't make plans for tomorrow night. My parents are leaving for Ireland in the morning so I'm having a party," Jake said. "See you in the morning, love you." Jake hung up quickly.

Love you. He'd said the words so casually. As if he always said them. But he didn't. *I* always said them, but half the time he didn't reciprocate. Did it matter?

Pushing my phone back onto my side table, I rolled over again and fell asleep. I could deal with my insecurities in the morning.

I was woken by the roar of Jake's truck in my driveway bright and early. *Crap.* I thought I'd overslept, but it was only five fifty.

Jumping out of bed, I tripped over a sweatshirt only to wind up flat on the floor. I lay there for a minute, and Jake's boots thudded on the staircase. I grabbed the sweatshirt and yanked it over my head as I stood. Jake knocked on the door and let himself in.

"Hey, sorry I'm early. I had to get away while my parents packed the car. I can't stand how wound-up dad gets when they're going away." Jake let out a huff of air as he collapsed on the bed. I climbed back into bed next to him and put my hand up to his face. The stubble of his beard coming in tickled my palm.

"Forget about your dad." I kissed him slowly, and then pulled back. "Who's coming to the party tonight?"

"Everyone," Jake grinned. "Well, everyone who's worth inviting."

"Well, I'm glad I was invited then!" I joked. Before I started dating Jake, I was never on that list of people *worth inviting*. I usually went with Zac to his friends' parties. Jake's group of friends mixed with them a little, but not much.

I first hung out with Jake before the beginning of my sophomore year; after I'd become good friends with a girl named Jessie. We stopped being friends soon after school began, though. I saw her at a lot of Jake's parties still, but Jessie always pretended she didn't know me, which I was totally okay with.

Jessie was one of the people who was friends with my group of friends, and Jake's group of friends. I tagged along with her to one of Jake's parties and it was the first time I'd ever got *really* drunk. The first time I'd ever had a drink at all for that matter. Not one of my prouder moments. In fact, some of the details of that night were still fuzzy...

"*Wanna go to this party with me tonight?*" *Jessie asked, sitting cross-legged across from me on my bed.*

"*Umm, I don't know. Whose party is it?*" *I asked, unsure whether I should go, knowing there would be a lot of people I didn't normally hang out with.*

"*Jake Williams. He's super-hot.*" *Jessie nudged me with her elbow. "And he broke up with his girlfriend, he's gonna need some help getting over her." She winked.*

"*I would feel weird going to his party, I've only talked to him once!*" *I tried to use this as an excuse, but Jessie wasn't giving up that easily.*

"*There are gonna be like fifty people there, I'm sure he won't even see you all night. Unless you want him to.*" *She winked again. I rolled my eyes and laughed with her.*

"*Fine. I'll go,*" *I agreed. I'd been crushing on Jake for a while anyway. Maybe this was my chance to finally have a real conversation with him.*

Jessie squealed with delight.

"*Maybe we should invite Zac,*" *I suggested.*

Jessie shook her head. "It's not his crowd. Besides, you don't want Jake to think you're with Zac. It's going to be so much fun! I already have our outfits planned and everything!"

That night, we went to Jessie's house.

"*Are you ready for this?*" *Jessie grinned as she went into her closet and out came the miniskirts and heels. "Dun duh-duh dun!"*

"*Wow.*" *I gaped at the clothes, or lack thereof. "Cute!" I feigned excitement at wearing the most revealing, uncomfortable outfit I'd ever worn.*

"*Let's get ready!*" *Jessie threw my outfit on the bed next and started changing into hers. It wasn't so bad. She had me wear a pink halter top that had a low back.*

Once we were ready to go, Jessie drove us to the party. When we walked through the front door, I knew it was going to be an interesting night. There were already drunk upperclassmen passed out on the couches. Jessie grabbed some drinks, which she claimed were "only slightly alcoholic," but they burned my throat as I drank and felt tipsy after one glass.

"I see someone I want to make out with. You good by yourself?" Jessie didn't even wait for my response before walking toward the kitchen.

I grabbed myself a beer and found a seat away from everyone else by the pool. There were plenty of people in the pool, but I was not up for that. Sitting by myself turned out not to be such a good plan. I wound up thinking about Zac and how he would never approve of me being there. I grabbed another one of those strong drinks to try to drown out my thoughts. There was some commotion inside and I went to check it out.

A group surrounded a small round table lined with shot glasses and someone was pouring vodka into each of them.

"Step right up and take a shot!" the guy shouted.

I recognized him from school. A couple of girls grabbed a shot and threw them back. I decided it was time I took my first shot.

"Well, hello there gorgeous! Come to take a shot? Here, this one's for you." The same guy who was pouring the shots passed one to me and I grinned at him, quickly downing it before I changed my mind. "Come on, have another!" I accepted the next shot he pushed my way, and soon, Zac was completely forgotten.

I found myself laughing hysterically as I watched some poor girl trying to flirt with a guy, but he walked away without giving her a second glance. The girl turned to glare at me, and I couldn't stop laughing, even though I felt horrible. The girl flipped her hair and stalked away. I moved as I realized I had to go to the bathroom but stumbled backwards and fell to the floor.

"Oof." I waited until the room stopped spinning and tried to get up.

"Hey, looks like you need a little help." A cute guy helped me up off the floor and steadied me. He had a charming smile, pretty eyes, cute hair, and... I covered my mouth. He seemed to understand what that meant and hurried me to the bathroom.

I hovered around the toilet for a while, but nothing came up. I leaned back and saw that the cute guy was still with me.

"Well, hello." I grinned, wanting him to come closer, even though I was on the verge of throwing up. One of the perks of being that drunk; I couldn't care less what people thought of me. "I'm Alana."

"That's a pretty name, Alana." He smiled back at me. Goosebumps pimpled my arms when he said my name. It sounded amazing coming from him. "How are you feeling?" Concern wrinkled his brow.

"With you? Amazing. My stomach, not so great." I gave him my best flirty smile, and then threw up in the toilet. He quickly gathered my hair and held it back.

The rest of the night we stayed in that position, occasionally readjusting to get comfortable. He chatted with me, keeping my mind off of the churning in my stomach. The party was dying down around three in the morning, which was when the cute guy left for a few minutes. When he came back, he had someone else with him.

"Alana? You still hanging in there?" he asked sweetly. I nodded. "Good. This is Jake, he's going to let you stay until you feel better and take care of you now, because I have to head home."

"I want you to take care of me." I meant for that to be directed at my new cute friend, but he didn't respond.

"I'll come check up on you. If you need anything just holler," Jake said, and they both left me alone in the bathroom.

I fell asleep for a few hours on the bathroom floor and woke when Jake came to check on me around nine in the morning. My stomach felt a little better, but I had a pounding headache.

"Hey, do you think you can make it home now? My parents are going to be home soon." Jake came and knelt beside me.

"Yeah," I rasped. My throat and mouth felt like sandpaper. Jake helped me up off the floor and into the kitchen. He sat me down on one of the bar stools and grabbed me a glass of water.

"Here, these will help." He placed two aspirins in front of me and I took them gratefully.

"I'm really sorry. I don't usually get this drunk, I swear," I said, turning bright red, not bothering to mention the fact that I'd never had a drink before.

"It's fine, people end up crashing here all the time." Jake shrugged, grinning. "It's not usually anyone as beautiful as you." I smiled but avoided meeting his eyes. I vaguely remembered flirting with someone else the night before as well. I wondered if I would ever see him again. I couldn't remember his name and his face was already blurring in my memory. Maybe it had been Jake the whole time.

"So, you're the one who took care of me last night?" I asked, trying to bring into focus the fuzzy image of the boy who held my hair back.

"Yeah, that was me," Jake answered. "So, you ready to go home?"

"Definitely." I took one last sip of water and slowly got off the bar stool. Jake helped me outside, seeing as I couldn't walk straight. As we reached his truck, I scrunched my nose at how far I had to climb to get inside.

"Don't worry, I've got you." Jake seemed to guess my worry and lifted me into his truck in one swift movement.

Zac waited for me in my living room when we arrived at my house. I could tell he was antsy about something. He could barely stand still.

"Where were you last night, Ally?" he asked. "Wait, before you say anything. I love you."

"Wait... You what?" I couldn't believe what I was hearing, and was unsure whether I was still dreaming, passed out on that bathroom floor.

"I love you, Alana," he repeated.

I'd always dreamed this would happen, but now it felt all wrong.

"I- ah. I don't know what to say." I smiled awkwardly, and then ran to the bathroom and threw up. I walked back to the entryway where Zac waited. "I am so sorry. I'm a little hungover," I admitted sheepishly.

"Oh. Maybe I should go." Zac left in a hurry, and I ran after him only to realize Jake was still in my driveway. Zac looked at the truck and there was hurt in his eyes as he glanced back at me before walking back to his house.

Jake got out of his truck.

"Hey, is everything okay?" he asked. I shook my head. "You want a ride out of here?" I nodded.

I told him all about Zac, and by the end of the day, we knew almost everything about each other's lives. That Monday when we were back at school, Jake introduced me to his friends. Then, when we hung out after school, he asked me to be his girlfriend.

Now, there we were, lying in my bed talking about another party at his house. They happened every time his parents went away, which was quite often.

"I should get ready for school." I pulled away from him reluctantly and grabbed some clothes, heading to the bathroom to shower. When I came back, Jake was asleep. I crawled back into bed with him. He draped an arm over me and pulled me closer. I breathed deeply and was soon asleep.

A little while later, Jake shook my shoulder.

"Come on, babe. Time to go." Jake stood up.

"I want to sleep forever." I put my pillow over my head. Jake's arms wrapped around me, and he lifted me out of bed. I laughed and tried to cling to my blankets. "No! I don't want to go!" Laughing, I squirmed in Jake's arms.

"Come on sleepy head, time for school." Jake carried me out of my room and down the stairs.

"I kind of like this, I could get used to it. Never having to walk anywhere, being carried around all day." I had my arms around his neck. He placed me back on my feet.

"I don't think so, princess." Jake chuckled and kissed the top of my head. Jake's phone beeped and he looked at the screen quickly. "I gotta go. Sorry, babe." He walked to the front door.

I stood, baffled, where he had left me.

"Excuse me?" I finally said. "How am I supposed to get to school? It's too last minute to get a ride from Mariah!" It was seven thirty, everyone else was probably already at school.

"I said sorry. I have things to do today. No time for school." Jake left the house and I remained rooted to my spot.

After a few minutes, I heard honking outside. Thinking Jake had come back, I hurried to the window, but it was Mariah sitting in the driveway. I sighed and grabbed my backpack before hurrying out to the car.

"How'd you know I would need a ride?" I asked, even though I already knew the answer.

"Lucky guess," Mariah shrugged.

I told her about the party.

"You want to come with me?" I asked.

"You mean: do I want to be your DD?" Mariah grinned. "Of course! I couldn't miss seeing you tripping over yourself every second!" I pushed Mariah playfully.

"Shut up! That has never happened. Besides, we don't need a DD. We can stay at Jake's tonight; I already ran it by him," I lied, but he owed me.

"Good, but I'm still not drinking. Who else will keep you out of trouble?" We both laughed. Our argument was behind us.

Once the final bell rang that day, I met Mariah at her car, and we drove to her house.

"What shall we wear tonight?" I was going through Mariah's closet while she lounged on her bed.

"Something spectacular of course! How else am I going to catch the eye of my next potential suitor?" Mariah always knew how to make me laugh.

"What about this?" I held up a sparkling black ruffle top along with a red mini skirt. Mariah hopped off her bed to inspect the outfit.

"I'll take the top, but I'm wearing jeans." Mariah took her outfit and went to the bathroom to get ready. While she was gone, I picked out an outfit for myself.

I pulled on one of Mariah's dresses. It was a simple black, tank-top dress that barely covered my butt. It didn't help that Mariah was a size smaller than me and a few inches shorter, but I sucked in my stomach, and it fit. Mariah came back into the room and twirled.

"How do I look?" she asked.

"Gorgeous, of course! What about me?" I twirled, too.

"Almost perfect. Hold on." Mariah pulled out two pairs of heels from her closet, a pair of black pumps for herself, and a pair of red pumps for me. I wasn't used to wearing heels, and nearly broke my ankle putting them on.

"K, now let me do your hair." I gestured to the seat in front of Mariah's vanity, and she sat down. I curled Mariah's shoulder-length brown hair into ringlets and pulled it back into a low side-pony. Then it was my turn to sit in the chair.

Mariah straightened my hair. It reached the middle of my back straightened, and Mariah pulled it into a high ponytail, making a small poof in the front.

"I think, Miss Alana, that we are ready to wow the masses." Mariah put her arm out and I looped mine through it.

"I believe you are right, Miss Mariah. Shall we?" I gestured toward the door, and Mariah nodded. We went downstairs and said goodbye to Mariah's parents.

"Bye mom, bye dad." Mariah waved from the hallway into the living room.

"Bye girls! Have fun and be careful!" Mariah's mom called out. Her parents thought we were going out to dinner with some friends and sleeping over at my house. I didn't need any excuses for Dianna, since she probably wouldn't even notice I was gone.

Chapter Five
Zac

Walking through the halls at school my first day back was a new kind of torture. All I wanted to do was crawl inside my locker and never come out. As I walked through the atrium, everyone stared, but no one tried to talk to me. I kept my eyes on the floor, counting the steps to my locker so I wouldn't snap.

I'd much rather be out looking for Ally, but since we'd only just begun hanging out again, I really had no idea where to look for her. The few places we'd hung out when we were younger wouldn't make very good hideouts, if she'd run away. And the entire town had been searching for her since she'd been announced 'missing,' and had come up with nothing so far.

"Is it your first day back too?" Mariah asked, sniffling and wiping her eyes, which were already red and puffy. Her locker was beside mine.

"Yeah. It sucks." I slammed my locker shut with my good arm.

"I know. I heard you were questioned by the police." More tears spilled down her cheeks and she quickly wiped them away.

"Yeah, it wasn't too bad." I ran my hand through my hair and turned my gaze back to the floor.

"Mm," Mariah hummed in agreement. I assumed that meant she'd also been questioned. "They're questioning Katrina today."

"I didn't realize she'd been there," I said. "Well, I guess I don't know most of the people who were there, since I still can't remember anything."

"I think a lot of people are hoping Ally's still alive, even though it's already been forty-eight hours, and they say that after that it's highly unlikely for someone to be found alive." I winced, but Mariah continued talking. "I read through a bunch of the comments of her Facebook." She bit her bottom lip.

My arm ached from helping support my books, so I shifted the full weight of them to my good arm.

"I couldn't read any of them. Too many people being fake and putting on a show," I said.

"Hey guys!" Josh walked up beside Mariah and put his arm awkwardly around her. She shrugged his arm off and stepped to the other side of me. They had broken up two weeks ago. Josh glared at her for a second.

"Hey. What's up?" I tried to lighten the mood.

"Oh, you know, same old, same old." Josh shrugged.

"Well, I have to get to class. Bye, Zac." Mariah purposefully didn't say anything to Josh. She hurried away, her brown curls bouncing on her shoulders.

"She's still mad about the breakup." Josh rolled his eyes.

"Yeah. I guess so," I agreed.

"You doing okay?" The carefree tone disappeared, and Josh lowered his voice. "First day back and all."

I cleared my throat. "Uh, yeah. I have to get to class, see you around." If I started talking about Ally, I would lose my hold on my emotions, and I really didn't want to cry in front of the whole school.

The bell rang, but Josh grabbed my good arm.

"Zac, seriously, if you need to talk, I'm here," he said.

I lifted my shoulder. "I'm serious, I'm good. But thanks, man." I kept my head down on my way to class until someone bumped into me.

"Oops! Sorry!" A feminine voice said, laughing. "You know what they say about texting and walking."

I glanced to the side. A girl with ice-blonde hair and bright green eyes smiled at me. She put her hand on my arm and the touch seemed electrified.

"Are you okay?" she asked, smiling. She wasn't asking if I was okay because my friend was missing, she was asking because she'd almost bowled me over. It was kind of refreshing to have someone who wasn't looking at me as if I might break down at any second.

She cocked her head to the side and pursed her lips. "Well, I'll take that as a yes. I've got to get to class. Excuse me." She slipped past me into the classroom I'd been blocking.

She probably thinks I'm crazy, I realized. I'd stared at her and not said a word. I groaned inwardly and trudged onward to my class.

You don't have time for girls, Zac. You need to figure out where Ally is, I chided myself. She could be out there, waiting for someone to find her. I wouldn't be the one to let her down.

At the end of the day, I almost forgot about my therapy appointment. But Mom made sure to text me a reminder.

"Zachary." Dr. Ryan spoke softly, but with authority. She sat across from me in a soft, plush armchair that matched the one I sat in.

"It's Zac," I corrected a bit gruffly. I cleared my throat hoping to cover up for it.

"Zac. Why don't you tell me why you're here today." She studied me closely, but her gaze wasn't judging or pitying.

"My mom thinks I need help processing my best friend going missing, and not being able to remember the night she disappeared," I stated bluntly. I wasn't going to waste any time there.

Nodding, she wrote something down in her notebook.

"And what do *you* think?"

I twisted my hands in my lap. "I think I can process fine on my own." Maybe *fine* was a little of an overstatement, but I'd manage.

"I understand feeling that way, but we can give this a try. Tell me about this friend of yours."

I told her everything. How Ally and I had been friends since we were little, and then how we fell out of friendship after she started dating Jake, I left out the part about me telling her I loved her. It wasn't really relevant anymore. I didn't feel like that was true anymore. I loved her as a friend, but after she left me behind for Jake, something changed. I'd moved on.

"It seems like she meant a lot to you."

"She did. *Does.*"

"I can understand why your mother would think you should talk to someone. It's hard to lose someone so close to you in such a traumatic way. Our time is up for today, but I'm going to give you my card." She grabbed a card from her side table and held it out to me. "If you need to talk about anything, at any time, don't hesitate to call. It doesn't have to be regarding Ally."

It left me with a bad taste in my mouth that she had talked about Ally as if she were already declared dead. It was different when Dianna did it. I didn't trust her motherly instincts, since she and Ally hadn't exactly been close. Now a stranger was doing it, and it felt *wrong*.

I left without making another appointment, telling Dr. Ryan my mom would call for that, but I didn't plan on going back. With all the talking, not a single memory came back to me from the night Ally disappeared. I wasn't going to waste time in therapy when I could be actively trying to find her.

When I got home, I went onto Facebook. This time I was going to weed through the posts on Ally's page even if I wanted to scream at the people who pretended to know her.

RIP. We had English together and you always made me laugh. Tessa Wright. Again, someone assuming she was already dead. It made my blood boil. But I kept scrolling anyway.

I think I saw her walking into a gas station in Epping yesterday. Peter Clark.

We'll keep searching until we find you. So tragic that this would happen in our town. Kelly Bern.

I leaned back in my chair and groaned. This wasn't going to help me at all. I scrolled past a few more stupid theories and then paused when a picture popped up. Ally stood with Mariah by the tower at the park and they were both sticking their tongues out. The caption read: *I can't believe I took this picture only hours before you disappeared. Someone must know where you are. Come home Ally.*

Jake's ex-girlfriend Katrina had posted it. There were a couple more people I recognized in the background of the picture, too. They all went to our school.

I didn't know what to do with any of this information. I assumed that the police had already questioned all these people, so what use would it be if I tried to ask them what they knew?

Groaning, I put my head on my desk and let the cool surface calm my scrambling brain.

My phone vibrated, tickling my face. Without lifting my head, I pressed the answer button and put it on speaker.

"You up for some skateboarding?" Josh's voice came through the phone. "Few of us are headed there now."

The idea actually brought me some semblance of excitement. It was like my body needed a bit of my normal life back and yearned for the familiarity of the indoor skate park. It helped that Ally had spent a lot of her time there when we'd been friends, too, so I could pretend I was there to look for her. It wouldn't be her top choice of hideouts, if she truly had run away, but it also wouldn't *not* be a contender for her.

"Yeah. I'll meet you there."

We spent most of our free time at the skate park unless we were on the trails at Aaron's. I assumed Aaron would be one of the few Josh had mentioned.

My suspicions were confirmed when I pulled in and saw Aaron's truck. Michael still sat in his truck, seemingly on his phone. He waved to me as I walked inside. It was busier than usual, but I picked out Josh easily enough.

He and Aaron were standing beside the bowl watching someone else perform some kind of trick. I couldn't tell from so far away.

I jerked forward as someone clapped me on the back and I laughed as Michael strolled by.

"Good to see you," he said, grinning. "Watch that." He grimaced as he noticed my arm in the sling.

I shrugged. "I've skated with worse."

"No, you haven't. But I'm not your mom, do what you want." He kept moving toward our friends and I followed him.

It didn't surprise me that Michael hadn't mentioned Ally. He didn't do well with comforting others.

"See that? I've been trying that for *years,*" Aaron was saying when I walked up beside him. "Oh, hey Zac." He nodded his head at me and then continued talking. I didn't pay attention to what he was saying as I watched the people in the bowl.

Josh came up to my other side as Michael and Aaron took off. "You sure you're up for this?" He eyed my arm. "No one would blame you for sitting this one out."

"Honestly, I think I need this. Life's been out of control lately, and I need to do something I know. Something that makes me feel like *me.*"

Josh jerked his head toward the ramp at the other end of the park. "Wanna race?" He grinned. It was a game they'd started when they were little and knew nothing about skateboarding. They'd go to the top of a ramp and race to the end. They were the only two of their group who still indulged in the nostalgia of it every once in a while.

"Yeah, let's go." I shoved his shoulder, and he went to shove me back but then hesitated, pointing to my arm. "Good call." We both laughed as we walked to the ramp.

Riding down the ramp seemed to take weight off my shoulders. It was freeing. Until I blacked out.

I could have sworn I heard someone screaming my name, and before I knew what was happening, I was jolted back into the present. My board skidded out in front of me, and I slid down the last bit of the ramp on my knees.

Josh stopped his board and ran over to me.

"You okay?" he asked, looking me over.

I winced as I attempted to stand up. "Yeah... Got a little distracted I guess."

Josh helped me to my feet. "Maybe you should take a break. Clear your head."

"Yeah, you're probably right." I could still hear the girl screaming in my head. I figured it was from that night at the park. Maybe it was Ally, but it didn't sound like her.

My stomach growled and I realized I hadn't eaten since breakfast. The snack bar was open across the room, and I strode over to it.

A girl popped up from behind the counter and I stopped in my tracks, eyes widening. It was the same girl who had bumped into me at school.

"You look familiar," she said, tapping her chin. "We go to school together, right?"

"Um, er, yeah. Yeah school," I said.

"Oh! I remember now! Sorry about barreling into you earlier." She scrunched her nose. "Do you want something? Chips, a drink?" She waved her hand over the options.

"I guess I'll have chips," I answered. "And it's fine about earlier. I hardly noticed."

She dipped down to grab the chips from beneath the counter and held them out to me.

"You seemed a little out of it," she said, putting the chips down when I didn't take them. "Two dollars please."

"How long have you worked here?" I asked. I'd never noticed her there before.

"A couple weeks. Two dollars please," she repeated, she smiled and blinked rapidly trying to hint that I was forgetting we were in the middle of a transaction.

I pulled out my wallet and handed her the cash. "Sorry. It's been a long week." Taking the chips, I waved to her and started to walk away.

I turned back before I got too far and called back to her, "What's your name?"

"Adriane," she said. "Adriane Monroe."

Monroe. I wondered if she was related to Officer Monroe.

"I'm Zac." I left off my last name, figuring she'd see it splashed over all the headlines soon enough. *Zachary Martin, Person of interest,* or whatever they called it.

"Well, it's nice to officially meet you, Zac." She smiled.

I took a seat on a bench while I watched everyone else skating. Eventually, I decided it was probably a better idea if I left. After my fall I'd lost the spark that had made me want to come down here in the first place, so I said goodbye to my friends and headed home.

On the drive home, I left the radio off. The quiet after the cacophony of the skate park was a nice reprieve. But it also gave me time to think.

Who was there that night? Mariah. Jake. Katrina. Ally. Me. The only one I could cross off of my possible suspect list was Mariah. Everyone else had a motive, and as for me... I didn't even know. Maybe there was a good reason my brain had scrubbed those memories from my mind.

I slammed my hand against the wheel in frustration.

"I didn't hurt her," I ground out. "I wouldn't do that." *Would I?*

Driving past my street, I kept going to the park, pulling up along the curb. I was surprised to find Jake there, sitting on the sidewalk.

I hopped out of my truck and walked over to him. "Hey," I said.

Jake jerked his head in a nod but kept staring at the ground. After a long moment of silence, he sighed and said, "I miss her. The police told me someone said there were rumors going around that I cheated on Alana. I need you to know that I didn't do it. I never technically cheated on her." Jake sighed again.

I decided not to point out that *technically* didn't help his case.

"You didn't?" I asked instead, crouching down, and resting my elbows on my knees so I could be eye level with him.

"No. I mean, I had a moment with Katrina, but Alana and I were on a break. Katrina and I are friends. You should know that. She's in your group of friends, isn't she?"

My cheeks heated as my blood boiled. *A moment.* No matter what it was, it should have never happened. Since Ally and I hadn't been talking while she was with Jake, I had no way of knowing if they'd ever actually taken a break, so I couldn't be sure if Jake was telling the truth, but unless Ally was miraculously alive, I would have to take his word for it. But I wouldn't condone what he'd done.

"I don't talk with her much," I said.

Jake went on. "Anyways, I loved Alana way too much to let her go. I guess that doesn't matter now, though." He laid back and stared at the clouds.

As much as I hated to do it, I decided to give him some comfort. "Ally loved you, too, if that's any consolation. I wasn't close with her for a while, but I at least knew that much." *Or else she never would have put up with you for so long,* I added silently.

I ducked under the crime scene tape to go onto the playground.

"What are you doing?" Jake asked. "That tape is there for a reason, so no evidence is compromised."

"They've probably gathered all the evidence by now and forgotten to take down the tape," I pointed out.

I went to the swings and Jake followed, sitting on the one beside mine.

"We got in a fight that night," he said. "That's why I wasn't there when... You know... It happened. I confronted her about wanting to get back together, but she was still upset. So, I walked away. That was how I left her. I didn't even tell her I loved her."

I didn't know how to respond to that. If what he was saying was true, that eliminated one more suspect from my list. Which meant I needed some more people to add to it.

"Who else was there that night?" I asked. "I still can't remember."

Jake narrowed his gaze at me but then shook his head. "A bunch of people from school. Katrina, Mariah, me, Joe,

Serena. I don't know. A handful of others. Sorry, but it's all kind of a blur."

I hadn't expected to get too much out of him. He was probably grieving too and didn't want to dwell on it.

We said our goodbyes and went our separate ways. I went straight upstairs to bed after dinner when I got home. Mom peppered me with questions about therapy while I ate, but I told her it was fine, and I made a follow up appointment for the next week. She didn't know that I wasn't actually going. I didn't want her to worry about me.

I dreamt of Ally that night.

*"Let me think... Nope. I can't remember. What is it?"
Ally asked.*

"I don't know. I was hoping you could remember his name. I've only met him once or twice." I laughed.

"Well, what are we supposed to do? Here he comes, shush." Ally tried to hide her smile as he reached us.

"Hey Alana, hey Zac. Are you ready to start our project?"

Of course, he remembered our names. Now I felt worse.

"Yeah, let's work out in the hall." Ally led the way into the hallway, and we sat against the lockers. "Do you want to write all our names on the poster?" she asked the boy whose name we couldn't remember, and she winked at me.

"I don't have that great of handwriting."

"Who cares, here use my pen." She gave him her pen, and he wrote our names on the poster. Once he finished, Ally said, "Thanks, Jonathan. Your writing isn't that bad. It looks great!" Ally struggled to hold back her laughter, but then a blush reddened her cheeks.

*I turned to see Jake standing down the hall at his locker.
"Do you think he'll notice me?" Ally whispered to me.*

"No offense, Ally, but I don't think he notices anyone except his girlfriend," I whispered back.

"Girlfriend? I can still look at him. Those luminous blue eyes... Oh! Here he comes!" She pretended to be working as he walked by. He smiled at her and I rolled my eyes. Ally was always so dramatic when it came to other guys.

"Hey, Jake. I didn't notice you were in the hall," she said coolly.

"Alana, right?" he asked.

"Yeah. We have study hall and math together." Alana blushed again.

"Well, I guess I'll see you around." Jake continued walking down the hall and Alana stared after him.

"I could melt..." She sunk further down onto the floor.

I woke up to a knock on my door. Rubbing my eyes, I checked the clock. It was seven in the morning, but it was Saturday. No need to get up so early. There was another knock on the door.

"Come in." I sat on the edge of my bed and Mom poked her head into my room.

"Breakfast's almost ready," she said.

"K," I mumbled.

I took a shower to try to wash away the memory my dream had brought back from freshman year. After, I went to the kitchen and sat at the bar while Mom finished making breakfast. Dad had already left for his business trip, so it would be the two of us for the next two weeks.

I knew Dad had to go on the trip so we could afford the lawyer, but I still wished he could stay and help me get through this whole ordeal.

"You have a doctor's appointment Monday to get your arm and head checked," Mom reminded me. "Can you get yourself there?"

"Yup." I twisted myself around on the barstool, debating whether I should ask Mom her thoughts on Ally's disappearance.

She placed a plate of pancakes in front of me. "Something on your mind?" she asked.

"Well," I huffed, about to tell her everything rattling around in there, but something stopped me. *What if she thinks you're responsible? You* are *the one Ally went to the park with that night.* I clenched my jaw. "Not really."

"Have you had any luck recovering any of your memories?" she asked, sitting on the stool beside me in front of her own plate of pancakes.

"Nope," I lied. It wasn't like I'd remembered anything of use. If I remembered something important, then maybe I'd tell her. But I wasn't going to recover any memories sitting in my kitchen.

After breakfast I went to the park. If anyone was watching me, they'd probably think I was guilty because of how often I was coming back to the scene of the crime. Some kind of sociopath wanting to relive the moment, or something like that.

I shuddered.

The crime scene tape had been removed, but there was still a stray piece that had been caught in a tree, reminding anyone who saw it what had happened there.

As I'd learned when I came to the park with Dad, the park wasn't where Ally had been shot. It was down by the pond beyond the trees. And there was no way to know if she had been shot, it was an assumption from the reports of nearby neighbors hearing a gunshot the night Ally disappeared. And the large amount of blood where they assumed it happened.

Too many facts to keep ignoring.

I walked the path that led to the pond. Bushes tugged at my pants on either side of the narrow path. You couldn't see the pond from the park because of all the trees. It was like a mini forest in the middle of suburbia.

Kind of like a slideshow, images of the path flashed through my mind, but it was dark, and I was moving faster. Yelling caught my attention, but I couldn't hear what was being said. And then I tripped over a branch and got stuck back in the present as I fell.

My arms went out on instinct, but with one in a sling, it didn't end well. I landed on my injured arm, and I cried out in pain, cursing as I rolled over and took the weight off it. Something dug into my back, but I ignored it, too focused on the pain in my arm.

"Hello?" A familiar, feminine voice called out. "Zac, is that you?" Mariah jogged toward me from the park.

"I'm here," I gasped, slowly catching my breath. "I'm fine." I sat up and hissed from the pain.

Mariah reached me and crouched down, putting a hand under my good elbow.

"Let me help you," she said.

Once I was back on my feet, the pain slowly ebbed away, though it didn't go away completely.

"What were you doing?" she asked, looking around like she might see someone else waiting for me.

I glanced toward the pond but shook my head.

"Nothing. It's stupid."

Mariah walked with me back to the park and we sat on the swings.

"It's not stupid," she said. "I know what you're feeling. You want answers."

"About that," I started, debating whether I should tell her about my flashbacks. Shaking my head, I decided against it. "Never mind, I don't even know how to go about finding answers."

"You can tell me anything, you know. I won't judge you, or whatever. If that's what you're worried about."

I nodded and smiled. "I know. With everything I've been told, and from what little I do remember, there were a lot of people here the night Ally disappeared. If she really was shot, then how does no one know what happened? Wouldn't *someone* have seen or heard something?"

Mariah twisted away from me on her swing. "I don't know. Like I said, I was gone before it happened."

Right.

A group of young kids walked onto the playground, so we took that as our cue to leave.

"Do you want me to walk you home?" I asked. Mariah lived in the opposite direction of my house, but I didn't mind a little extra time out of the house.

She shook her head. "I'm okay, thanks. See you later."

I took my time walking home, despite the air growing cooler as the sun descended. I thought of all the times I'd walked Ally home. It almost felt like that had never happened. As though all the time I'd spent with her had been a dream. I could hardly remember all her features anymore. All I had left were pictures and quickly fading memories.

Chapter Six
Alana
Nine days before

Once we reached Jake's house, it was dark, and his yard was filled with cars. It seemed like he lived in the middle of nowhere because his house was surrounded by woods and there were no other houses for a mile.

Mariah turned off her car and stared out her windshield at the people going into Jake's house. There were girls wearing much less clothes than we were in the forty-degree weather. Jake had a heated pool in his backyard. They only closed it when there was snow on the ground.

"Well, I'm glad to see we're not overdressed," Mariah commented. I nodded and got out of the car. Mariah came around to stand beside her. "You okay?"

I took deep breaths looking up at Jake's house. I thought about what had happened that morning. Why he had left my house in such a hurry and why he was so reluctant to tell me where he'd been going.

"Yeah, fine." I forced a smile.

There were so many people inside and I couldn't pick out anyone I knew well enough to talk to. We squeezed by a group of sophomore girls and made our way to the back of the house. Once we reached the kitchen, we found some of Jake's friends.

"Hey, Alana," Joe greeted me.

"Hey Joe, you remember my friend Mariah?" I pulled Mariah into the room. Joe had been interested in Mariah the first time they'd met at one of Jake's other parties. And I figured Mariah might need someone to get her mind off of her breakup with Josh.

"Of course I do!" Joe grinned.

"Ally!" Jake's friend Hannah came out of nowhere and hugged me. "You look so cute! I can't believe this party, one of Jake's best I must say," Hannah yelled over the music.

I nodded and smiled. Hannah was one of those girls that pretended to be best friends with everyone but then talked badly about them behind their backs.

"Come on, Mariah, let's go find my boy." I winked at Joe and led Mariah away, leaving Hannah behind. There were people that I'd never met filing through Jake's door. I recognized a lot of them from school.

I spotted Connor outside by the pool and headed in that direction. When I reached him, Jake had joined him. I put my arms around him from behind and laughed as he jumped. He turned to me and grinned.

"Hey beautiful." Jake kissed me and turned back to Connor, keeping his arm around my shoulders. "We were debating going for a swim."

"Would you like to join us, ladies?" Connor asked, looking back at Mariah.

"Do you have any idea how long it took for me to do her hair?" I motioned to Mariah's perfect curls, and she laughed.

"It's fine, you can go. I'll sit here." Mariah sat down on one of the many lawn chairs lining the pool.

"Well, I'm not going in without you!" I sat beside her. "You boys have fun; we'll stay dry and warm out here." I gave

Jake a little push toward the pool. Jake shrugged, and both him and Connor stripped down to their boxers and jumped into the water. A few drops of water landed on me.

"Hey, watch it!" I yelled at them jokingly.

"Babe come here for a sec." Jake waved me over to the side of the pool. I approached him warily as he pulled himself out of the pool, dripping wet.

"Don't trust him, Ally!" Mariah laughed.

There was a spark of mischief in Jake's eyes. I turned back to Mariah, and Jake ran up behind me and picked me up.

"No! Stop, Jake!" I tried to get free, but he jumped backwards into the pool with me still in his arms. Connor and Mariah broke out laughing as I resurfaced.

Pushing down on Jake's shoulders, I forced him under water, but he quickly came back up.

"You jerk." I couldn't stay mad at him. I swam to the edge of the pool and put my shoes there. Jake came up behind me again and whirled me around.

"Aren't you glad that you decided to come for a swim?" Jake smirked.

"Why don't you come in, Mariah?" Connor called up to her. Mariah slipped off her heels and sat on the edge of the pool with her legs dangling in the water.

"I'm okay over here," Mariah said.

"I should be getting back to the party," Jake said. He gazed through the doors into the living room.

I pushed myself away from him.

"Fine. Go back," I huffed, crossing my arms.

Jake rolled his eyes and pulled me close again.

"Don't be like that. I'm the host, I have to do my hosting duties," he tried to reason with me, but I'd already seen who'd walked in the front door: Katrina.

"I said fine." I pushed him away.

Jake gave up and pulled himself out of the pool. I lay back and drifted in the water for a few moments with my eyes closed. Mariah was by my side when I opened them.

"Decided to take a swim?" I asked.

"Yeah. I figured what the heck, my hair can look like this any day, but how often do I get to swim with my best friend, fully clothed, in the middle of fall?" Mariah laughed, clearly trying to cheer me up. I tried to smile, but I could see Jake making his way toward Joe and Katrina. I knew he wasn't going over there to talk with Joe. Connor was walking up the steps out of the pool.

"Connor?" I called out to him.

He turned back to look at me, a question in his eyes. "Yeah?"

"Will you stay with us?" I asked, hoping he wouldn't think I was using him to make Jake mad, even though I kind of was. Connor smiled and walked back into the water. As he made his way over to us, a couple groups of people walked out to the pool. Some people jumped in, while others sat down on the lounge chairs.

We stayed in the pool for a while longer, and then decided to go back into the house. Of course, Mariah and I were drenched. Luckily, I had a drawer of clothes in the guest room. We changed into some of my clothes, fixed our makeup which had been completely washed off in the water, and rejoined the party.

"Do you think anyone would notice if we egged the house?" Mariah asked, smirking.

I nudged her with my elbow. "You know they would. Though I'd love to see Jake have to clean up that mess."

"I might want to see that too," a familiar voice said from behind us. We both whipped around and came face to face with Katrina smiling at us. "Sorry, didn't mean to eavesdrop."

I couldn't help the scowl that curled my lips as my stomach dropped.

"Where's Jake?" I asked, trying to keep the jealousy out of my voice.

Katrina cocked her head. "Not sure. I haven't seen him since I came in. He said 'hi,' then headed for the kitchen."

Mariah tugged on my arm, and we moved away from Katrina.

"Wait," Katrina's hand wrapped around my wrist lightly. "I want to let you know, there's nothing between Jake and I anymore. Connor said something about it, and I didn't want you to think I was shady or anything. If Jake is letting you believe there's something there, then that's on him."

Pausing, I considered Katrina's explanation. It made sense, I didn't think she was the kind of girl to do that, but that would mean that Jake was purposefully trying to make me jealous, and I wasn't sure I wanted to believe that either.

Without responding, I let Mariah lead me away to a corner where we could recoup and figure out our next move.

The rest of the night Jake didn't talk to me, so I couldn't try to talk to him about what Katrina had told me. Mariah and I left around midnight to go back to my house. I hardly got any sleep, thinking about Jake and Katrina, and whether I could trust her.

I tried calling Jake the next morning, but his mom answered his phone.

"Bette, hi!" Jake's mom was like a second mom to me since Dianna didn't seem to take much interest in my life.

"Ally, dear! It's so nice to talk to you! I'm afraid Jake left his phone at the house again," Bette said.

"I thought you were in Ireland?" I asked. They had only left the morning before.

"Change of plans. You know Jake's dad, always getting last-minute business calls. We stayed at a hotel last night and came home this morning. It was a bit of a mess around here, but Jake cleaned it up quite nicely. I don't suppose you had anything to do with that?" Bette asked. She didn't really care whether Jake had parties, so long as he cleaned up afterwards.

"No, not me," I teased, making Bette laugh. "Could you let Jake know I called when he gets back?"

"Of course, darling! Will you come to visit soon? It seems like I haven't seen you in weeks!" Bette was right; I hadn't seen her in almost a month. Jake wasn't inviting me over as often.

"I will! I promise, even if I have to force Jake to let me come over," I laughed, but knew that it may come to that.

"You can come over whenever you like. In fact, Jake's dad and I are having a little last-minute dinner party tonight if you would like to come," Bette offered.

"I would love to! I'll see you then!" Bette said goodbye and hung up. Mariah watched me from her bed made from comforters on the floor. "What?" I asked.

"No Jake?"

"No Jake, but I'll see him tonight. Bette invited me to a dinner party at their house. Which means dinner with Jake's older sister." Jake had one sibling, his older sister, Caroline. Sometimes I wasn't sure whether Caroline liked me or not. She was the only other person besides Connor and I who knew about Jake's terrible relationship with his dad. His mom liked to pretend they had the perfect family and ignored all the arguing.

"Let's get some breakfast," Mariah said, holding her hand out to me. I took it and we went in search of food.

That night I got ready for the dinner party thinking about whether Clyde had told Dianna about my dad calling. Definitely not. Maybe he had stopped calling. Maybe he would stay out of our lives. The phone rang as I was about to walk out the front door as if I'd jinxed herself.

"Hello?" I answered the phone.

"Is this my Ally?" I could hear the happiness in his voice, and I hated it. He had no right to be happy after leaving us.

"No. This is not your Ally. I really can't talk, I'm going out. Goodbye." I hung up and ran out the door before he could call again. No one else was home so I didn't have to worry about anyone else answering the phone. I tried to put my dad out of my mind as I drove to Jake's house. Clyde was letting me borrow his car for once.

Bette opened the door when I rang the doorbell. She grinned and ushed me in.

"Ally, dear! Come inside."

Caroline and Jake sat in the living room watching TV while their dad was in the kitchen, sitting at the bar. "I have to get back to cooking, but you go join Jake and Caroline in the living room." Bette went back to the kitchen, chatting with Robert.

I hesitantly walked over to the couch.

"Ally! It's so nice to see you!" Caroline patted the cushion beside herself. "Sit!"

I did as she said and sat down. Jake said nothing to me as we watched TV; he didn't even look at me. I tried to guess what he was so mad about this time. I assumed it was the mere fact of my presence when he hadn't invited me.

"Dinner!" Bette finally called from the dining room. After we were all seated, we were allowed to start eating. "So, Caroline, how is your new boyfriend? Chase, was it?" Bette never liked any of Caroline's boyfriends. I assumed that was part of the reason that Caroline was on the edge of liking *me*. Bette had never had any problem with me.

"He's great, actually. Cory and I were thinking about moving in together," Caroline said, casually correcting Bette's obvious mistake, but putting extra emphasis on the name.

"That's great. I hope to be meeting him soon, honey," Jake's dad, Robert, commented and Caroline nodded.

"Yes. I hoped he would be able to come tonight, but he had to stay late at work. He works over at the hospital, you know. He's in the residency program," Caroline informed them.

"That's lovely!" Bette exclaimed, smiling brightly.

Robert looked at Jake, disappointment in his eyes. I knew that look well, since he gave it to Jake almost every time they were together.

"Doctors are nice, but they work long hours. I don't think I'd be okay with being home alone all that time," I interjected. "I'd be happy with a mechanic, personally." Jake smiled knowingly, since that was exactly what he hoped to become.

Caroline sighed heavily, and Robert scoffed. "Mechanics make no money. Especially in this town," he grumbled.

"Money is not the most important thing in life," I said. "I think that as long as my family is happy and healthy, I don't need to be rich."

"Wait till the bills start rolling in," Robert murmured.

Why does he have to be so frustrating? Couldn't he accept that his son wanted to be a mechanic and move on with his life? I groaned inwardly.

"Robert, honey. I think that's enough. Alana here knows what she's getting herself into. I don't think she needs a lecture from you on money," Bette said, trying to ease the tension in the room.

"That's right, dad. I know all about it too, and I don't need your constant reminder that being a mechanic isn't good enough for you. Why can't you shut up about it?" Jake pushed back from the table and stormed out of the room.

"Another one of his temper tantrums," Robert chided.

"No, he's right! Nothing he does is good enough for you! Just like no one I date is good enough for mom!" It was Caroline's turn to storm out of the room.

"What has gotten into these kids?" Robert shook his head.

"I have no idea." Bette shrugged, completely oblivious to the fact that Caroline had been trying to make a point to her.

"I should probably check on Jake." I pushed back from the table and fled the room. I found Jake in his room. He was fuming as he paced back and forth in front of his window.

"Jake?" I approached him cautiously.

"You should leave," Jake snapped at me.

"No."

He whipped around. "Damn it, Ally! Can you leave? Please? I never asked you to come tonight! I don't want you here!" Jake's face was bright red.

I stepped back, hurt that he would take all his anger out on me, but unwilling to leave him alone.

"No. Jake, I love you and I am not leaving you." I stood my ground.

"Saying you love me is not going to make anything better. It's not going to change the way my dad looks at me. It's not going to change anything. Get the hell out of my house," Jake spat.

I backed away from him toward the door. His resentment should not have shocked me, this had all happened before. In fact, dinners with his family almost always ended with everyone storming out, and then me trying to comfort Jake. He had developed the habit of brushing me aside. Nothing ever changed, why should I expect it to now?

"Fine. I'm leaving." I opened his bedroom door and, with great restraint, lightly shut it behind me. Something slammed against the wall, but I kept walking down the hall, down the stairs, and out the front door.

Chapter Seven
Zac

Monday morning, Mom was on her way out the door when I made it downstairs to the kitchen.

"I have to get to work; don't forget you have a doctor's appointment today at four thirty! See you later!" she said as she rushed out the door.

The day dragged on as I sat through class after class. Finally, the day ended, and I had some time to kill before my appointment, so I decided to go to the indoor skate park. Josh was busy, so I went alone.

Adriane was working at the snack counter again. I waved to her then climbed to the top of the skate ramp. There were only a couple other people there and I watched them for a few minutes before getting on my board. I was trying not to push my luck with my injured arm, so I didn't try any tricks.

I decided to take and break and headed for the snack bar.

"Hey, Adriane. How's it going?" I leaned onto the counter to stop myself from rolling.

"Living the dream," she smirked. "How are you doing? Need a snack?"

"Nah, I wanted to say hi. But I'm going to go back," I said, pointing with my thumb over my shoulder.

"Skateboarding." I pushed off from the counter, trying not to visibly cringe from my horrible attempt at flirting.

I chanced a look back over at Adriane and thank God she was smiling and not laughing at me. She waved, and I skated down into the bowl.

Air rushed past my face, but my vision blurred for a second, and I heard that screaming again. This time it sounded like someone was screaming my name. Then there was nothing and I felt the impact of the floor as I fell, face first, off my board. All the air rushed out of my lungs, and I gasped for air. My arm throbbed, and I tried to move, but my body screamed in protest. My skateboard hit my non-fractured arm when I fell and had cut my bicep. It bled through my shirt. I shifted, groaning in pain, to take my weight off my fractured, probably now broken, arm.

"Zac?" Adriane yelled. "Zac are you okay?" Her hurried footsteps were approaching the bowl. "Oh!" Adriane breathed. She slid down into the bowl and stopped beside me.

"Don't worry, worse has happened to me," I said breathlessly, trying to make light of my painful situation.

"I'm going to call 911. I don't think I should try to move you by myself. I'll be right back." She started to climb back up out of the bowl, but I grabbed her hand.

"No, don't do that. I'm okay, really." I used my good arm to push myself into an upright position. Adriane eyed me warily. "See?"

"I'm not so sure..."

"Here, help me up," I held my hand out to her.

Adriane helped me stand, grimacing when I cringed, and walked me to the side of the bowl.

"How were you planning on getting out of here?" she asked, grinning slightly. I had to admit, it would be comical if I weren't in so much pain.

"You go up first. I got this." Adriane looked me over and then climbed out of the bowl. She put her arm out for me to grab as I hauled myself up and over the edge. She closed her eyes as I kept wincing in pain.

"This is probably not helping your injuries at all," she said as I finally sat beside her with a huff.

"I was supposed to go to the doctor's today anyway."

"Yeah, I don't think they actually *want* you to come with more injuries," Adriane pointed out. "I'll drive you to the hospital. I can close the snack bar for a little bit." She helped me out to her car and got in the driver's seat. "Should I get used to your wipeouts here? I need to know so I can be prepared next time." She laughed.

My cheeks heated. I hadn't realized she'd seen me fall last time, too.

"No, I'm not having a good week is all." I laughed along with her but stopped shortly because it only caused more pain.

At the hospital, they bandaged up my arm that was bleeding, took some x-rays, and brought me into a room to await the doctor. Adriane had gone back to the skate park since she had to work, but she called my mom to let her know what had happened. That meant my truck would be at the skate park until I could get a ride to pick it up, but I didn't mind having the excuse to see Adriane again.

The doctor came in with his x-rays and told me that my fracture had become a full break and pointed out a couple big bruises down my right side that were already forming from my fall.

After about twenty minutes, Mom arrived at the hospital and hurried into the room.

"What did I tell you about skateboarding?" she exclaimed.

"That it's extremely safe and fun!" I grinned.

Mom glared at me.

The doctor also checked my head while I was there, but there was still no sign of damage. By the time I was in a cast and released, it was well after dinner time, so we drove through a fast-food place.

Mom let me sleep in the next day and stayed home from work.

"I figured you wouldn't want to go to school today considering." She gestured to my arm.

"Yeah. I can catch up with all my work tomorrow during my study hall." I grabbed a soda and headed for the front door. "I'm going out."

"No skateboarding!" Mom yelled after me.

I considered going back to the crime scene to try to jog my memory again, but something told me that wouldn't do it. So, instead, for the first time in as long as I could remember, I walked to the local library. It wasn't much farther than the school.

The library had computers I could use to look up local maps. I didn't have one at home, and my phone could be a hindrance for these kinds of projects.

Stepping into the library was almost like walking into a whole different world. The outside chaos quieted, and the smell of books overwhelmed any other scent. I greeted the librarian at the front desk and headed straight for the computers at the center of the main floor.

It wasn't too difficult to bring up the town maps. All I needed was a good one that showed all the wooded areas around. If I couldn't remember what happened to Ally, maybe I could at least find her, if she was truly dead. The thought made me shudder and nausea swirled in my gut.

As much as I wanted to believe Ally was still alive and well, there were too many things stacking up against that outcome.

I dug my nails into my palms at that thought. Thinking of her being dead almost felt like giving up on her, even though it was the most likely outcome. Going off all the crime shows I'd watched, a shallow grave in the middle of an unpopulated forest seemed like a good place to find a body.

Printing off a copy of the town map, I folded it up and stuck it in my pocket. I'd go over it more thoroughly at home, where there was no chance I'd be watched. I had to imagine it was suspicious for a suspect in an open investigation to be looking up town maps, regardless of their reasoning.

When I got home, I went over the map, highlighting all the best places to hide a body, mentally noting how this would look if the police found it, and making sure to tuck it away out of sight.

My phone vibrated on my desk, jolting me out of planning mode. *Mariah.* I don't think she'd ever called me before.

"Hello?" I answered hesitantly.

"Hey. What are you doing?" she asked.

I couldn't help but wonder if she somehow knew I'd been investigating, but I kept that to myself. "Nothing. Why?"

"This is weird for you, I'm sure. But do you want to hang out?"

"It's not *that* weird," I teased. "But sure. I've got nothing going on. Although I do need to go to the skate park at some point to pick up my truck."

"Well, I can drop you off. I'll be at your house in ten." She hung up.

When Mariah arrived, she plopped onto the couch beside me as if we'd done this every day for years. It was kind of nice, having someone around again like that. Josh and I were close, but not as close as Ally and I had been.

"You weren't at school today," she stated.

I glanced at her and noted the indifferent look on her face.

She continued, "You missed a fight in the parking lot."

"What?" I perked up. Of course, the one day I wasn't there something interesting would happen. There were hardly ever fights at our school.

"It was between Josh and Connor. Jake was there trying to break them up," Mariah sighed. "I don't know why they all have to be such hot heads."

"Why were they fighting?" I asked. It wasn't unusual for Josh to be quick to anger, but it was weird that he was interacting with Jake or any of Jake's friends. Maybe I missed a lot more than class work at school.

Mariah pursed her lips and turned her face to the ceiling as she leaned her head back on the couch cushion. "Not really sure. I saw it from the sidewalk."

"So weird." I tried to remember ever seeing Josh and Connor together at a party or in school. It could have been as simple as fighting over a girl. I wouldn't put it past Josh to get upset about something like that. But I didn't want to suggest it in front of Mariah since she used to date him. We weren't on that level of friendship yet, I didn't think.

"Oh my gosh!" Mariah's eyes grew wide as she noticed the cast on my arm. "What happened?"

"Skateboarding accident," I said.

Mariah cocked her brow but didn't pry for details, which I appreciated.

"So why did you want to hang out?" I asked.

She brought her knees up to her chest and wrapped her arms around them. "I don't know. I was bored and... Well, since Ally's been gone, I realized I don't really have many other friends. I figured you might be in the same boat and appreciate not being alone for a few hours." Though she avoided eye contact, I could still see tears glistening on the brim of them.

My gut twisted. She wasn't wrong, I did understand how she felt. But I'd also lost Ally once before, when she started dating Jake, and even though she'd been around at school, I'd come to terms with her not being in my life. The few days I'd had of being friends with her again had been a glimpse into what we could have again, but it still wasn't the same as it had been.

But it was nice to have someone to talk to about Ally that knew her as well as I did.

"It's been weird not seeing her at school. I half expect her to show up as if nothing happened," I said.

Mariah laughed. "Me too. I could have sworn I saw her this morning in the hallway, but it was some freshman who had the same dyed brown hair." She shook her head, leaning her cheek on her knee and looking over at me. "She did love you; you know?"

My breath caught in my chest, and I held it there.

Mariah continued, "She used to talk to me about a future where the two of you would get married and live in New York, or some other fancy city. She wasn't sure she wanted a family, so that would change whenever she talked about it, but you were the only consistent piece of her imagined future. Until Jake."

I wanted to let the couch suck me into it and never come out. Ally had never admitted to loving me, and when I'd told her I loved her, she immediately went off and started dating Jake. There was no part of me that thought she had ever loved me back. And I'd moved on.

"I'm sorry she never told you how she really felt. I think she was confused when you told her you loved her, and the easy way out was to start dating Jake. Don't get me wrong, she loved him too." She sighed and lifted her head. "I shouldn't have said anything. I'm probably making things worse."

I cleared my throat. "No. Thank you for telling me. It's nice to know that I wasn't crazy thinking we could be more than friends." Even if it would eat at me for a while, thinking about what could have happened if she had never started dating Jake.

"Do you want to go to the skate park and pick up my truck? Might as well get it over with." I changed the subject.

Mariah hopped off the couch as if she'd been waiting for a change of pace as well. "Yeah. Let's do it."

At the skate park, Mariah came inside with me so I could grab the keys from Adriane. Thankfully she was working, because I didn't have her phone number.

"Hey Zac! I'm glad you're okay. Sorry I couldn't stay at the hospital with you." Her gaze shifter to Mariah. "Oh, hi, I don't think we've met. I'm Adriane," she introduced herself.

"Mariah. Zac's friend."

"It's nice to meet you." Adriane smiled sweetly.

"I figured I should pick up my truck, and I wanted to thank you for driving me to the hospital," I said.

"Someone had to do it," she teased. "But it was no problem, really. It gets boring here, so it was nice to have a little excitement for the day." She winked.

Mariah nudged my arm with her elbow.

"When don't you work?" Mariah asked, leaning onto the counter.

"Well, I get out today at five, and I don't work tomorrow," Adriane said, her gaze flicking between me and Mariah. "Why?"

Instead of answering, Mariah kicked my ankle.

I sucked in a breath and turned to glare at her, but she kept her eyes on Adriane.

"Do you want to hang out with Zac and I tomorrow after school?" Mariah asked, shooting an annoyed look at me.

"Um, sure." She smiled and tucked a lock of her long blonde hair behind her ear. "Oh, and." She ducked below the counter and came back up with my keys in her hand, holding them out to me.

"Oh, yeah. The whole reason we're here," I joked. "Thank you."

"Well, we should let you get back to work, but we'll see you tomorrow," Mariah said, gripping my elbow. She turned us to the door, but I glanced back over my shoulder and said goodbye to Adriane.

Once we were in the parking lot where Adriane wouldn't hear us, I asked Mariah, "What was that about?"

"So, do you *not* like Adriane?" she asked, giving me an incredulous look. "Because I gave you a clear opening to ask her on a date, and you failed. You're welcome, by the way."

I gaped at her. "What are you talking about?" So maybe I liked Adriane and wanted to go on a date with her, but now was not the time.

Mariah groaned. "Look, I understand that you're grieving, because I am too. This whole situation sucks. But that doesn't mean we should stop living. Ally would want you to go on a date with Adriane. Heck, she would have kicked you twice as hard as I did in there."

The worst part was, she wasn't wrong. I could picture Ally doing exactly that.

"Fine. You're right," I admitted. "I like her, she seems cool. I want to go on a date with her."

"Perfect. You have a date with her tomorrow after school."

"You're going to be there tomorrow, so it won't be a date," I pointed out.

"I have a dentist appointment tomorrow, so I can't go. There. It's a date." Mariah laughed. "You should ask her out on a REAL date though, like this weekend. I have to go, though. Keep me updated." Mariah waved as she walked back to her car.

I drove home thinking about Adriane. I almost felt guilty that I was so excited to see her again. The only girl I'd ever really had feelings for as more than a friend was Ally. I wasn't sure I was ready to start falling for anyone yet after everything that had happened with her and with what Mariah had told me.

The next day, I waited for Adriane at the end of school in the atrium. She finally walked up to him as the last people cleared out of the school.

"Hey, sorry I took so long. I had to finish this project thing, it's dumb. You ready to go?" She had her backpack slung over one shoulder and her icy-blonde hair was falling out of the tie that held it up. I couldn't help but think about how beautiful she looked, and I flashed back to a memory of Ally, when we were in our weird, not friends, limbo stage.

Ally hurried past me in the hall with a dejected look on her face. Mascara streaked down her face and gave away the fact that she'd been crying. It appeared as if she'd tried to wipe it away but had given up on it. Her dyed brown hair was up in a messy bun, and she looked as beautiful as ever. I stood at my locker, thinking about reaching out to her, offering support. But she had been the one to end our friendship. She had decided to leave my words unanswered and run off with Jake.

As she passed, she glanced in my direction. Her face reddened and she turned it the other way.

"I'm fine," she muttered.

I pretended not to hear as I slammed my locker shut and stalked off in the other direction.

"Zac, you okay?" Adriane waved her hand in front of my face, trying to get my attention.

I snapped back to reality and shook off the memory. I couldn't help but wonder if I had reached out to Ally then, if things may have ended differently. Whether we would have become friends again sooner. Maybe I would have had more time with her. I pushed all those thoughts aside and focused solely on Adriane.

"Yeah, sorry. Let's go." We walked outside to my truck. "If it's all right with you, we're going to stop at my house first."

"Yeah, that's fine. Are we waiting for Mariah?" she asked glancing back at the school.

"Oh crap, I should have asked if it's okay if she's not here. She backed out at the last minute, and I should have told you, but I don't have your number. We can reschedule if you don't want to hangout-"

Adriane put up her hand, and smirked. "Zac, it's fine. It was only a question. I still want to hang out with you."

I bit my lip and shoved my hand through my hair. "Got it, sorry."

"Don't apologize. Let's just go." She brushed her arm against mine before walking to the passenger door and hopping into my truck. I realized I was staring and quickly followed suit, getting into the driver's side and starting up the engine.

"Are you okay with going for a walk to the park? There's not much else to do around here, and I'm sure you don't want to spend your free time at the skate park," I joked.

Adriane scrunched her nose. "You'd be right about that. That sounds fine. Anything is better than going home to do homework."

We left my truck at my house and walked toward the park. It was bright and sunny outside and almost felt like spring, even though we were in the thick of fall.

The crime scene tape had finally been removed from the perimeter of the playground. Adriane walked over to the seesaw and sat on one end.

"Seriously?" I asked, grinning.

"Yes, come on," she laughed.

"I haven't been on this thing in forever." I walked over and sat on the other end, pushing off from the ground.

"The seesaw used to be my favorite thing on the playground. My brother and I would sit on it all day, trying to see who could keep the other in the air longest." She smiled, and a single dimple on her right cheek appeared.

Ally had dimples, too.

Wait, don't think about her. I chided myself. *Although Adriane's father is the officer assigned to Ally's disappearance, maybe she has some information I don't.* NO. I had to yell at myself to stop the flow of thoughts.

"So, what did you do today at school?" Adriane asked, bringing me back to the conversation.

"Nothing of great importance, as usual. And you?"

"Same." There was an awkward pause. "But it's my birthday this Friday." She smiled. "The big one seven."

"Very nice. My birthday was October third." I stuck my legs out so I would stay on the ground and Adriane remained aloft in the air. I laughed as she tried to make her side of the seesaw go back down.

"Very funny. If you get off though..." She stopped as I pushed off from the ground. "Thank you." She laughed and then did the same thing to me. "When my brother and I would do this, one of us would eventually get bored and get off while the other was still up and send them crashing to the ground." She pointed to her elbow. "I have a scar from one such event."

"I'd much appreciate you not being as cruel to me," I joked. "Though, it does sound pretty entertaining."

She stuck her tongue out at me but pushed off from the ground.

"We should do something this weekend. You know, dinner or something. For your birthday," I suggested, pushing off and letting her back down to the ground.

"I'd like that." She pushed herself off the ground.

Once again, everything went black, and I heard that screaming again. The next thing I knew, I'd lost my balance and landed hard on the ground.

"Zac!" Adriane jumped off the seesaw and ran to me.

Once I could finally breathe again, I rolled onto my stomach and attempted to push myself up from the ground. Adriane grabbed my good arm and helped me.

I can't take this anymore. I was fuming, but I didn't want to yell and scare Adriane. I walked back to the street and toward my house. Adriane followed, trying to keep up.

"Are you okay, Zac?" She caught up with me and grabbed my arm. "Talk to me, please."

I pulled my arm away.

"I'm sorry. I'll take you home."

Chapter Eight
Jake
Eight days before

I slammed my fist against the wall. Why did my dad have to be such a dick? Alana's footsteps faded and I instantly regretted the way I'd treated her. It wasn't my fault though. She shouldn't have been so up in my face after making me look weak in front of my dad. I didn't need anyone to defend me.

There was a knock on my door. He debated ignoring it, but opened it, expecting it to be Alana. Instead, Caroline stepped in.

"Hey, Jakey. I'm sorry about Dad. He doesn't mean anything by it; he wants you to be successful," Caroline tried to defend our father, as usual, but I didn't want to hear it.

"Whatever. He's pissed that I'm not as perfect as you." I stormed past her, almost making it to the front door before my mother called me back.

"Jake, darling, please come into the kitchen. Your father and I would like to speak with you."

Ugh. Why does she have to call me 'darling?' I thought.

"What do you want?" I asked, slumping against the counter in the kitchen. My dad stood tall with his arms crossed, while my mother sat on one of the barstools with her best fake smile on. I rolled my eyes.

"I think we need to talk about your attitude problem, young man," my dad began. That was enough for me. I didn't need any of that; I'd already had the same talk with my dad about a million times. I strode out of the kitchen and to my truck before they could stop me.

I drove automatically to Alana's house but remembered that she probably hated me.

Where could I go? Connor's maybe, or Katrina's. No, not Katrina's. I couldn't do that to Alana... Could I? *No.* I would go to Connor's.

I pulled up outside Connor's house only to find that Connor wasn't home. Maybe if I went to Alana and begged her to forgive me... I turned around and headed in the direction of her house. As I drove down her street, I saw her walking along the sidewalk. I smiled, knowing that it was what she did when she was upset. Then I realized she was making her way up Zac's driveway toward where he stood with one of his friends. What was she doing?

I didn't want to see what would happen next, so I pulled a U-turn and headed over to Katrina's. If Alana could hang out with the guy who used to be in love with her, then why couldn't I hang out with my ex?

Chapter Nine
Zac

After driving Adriane home, I called Mariah. I guessed she was still at the dentist because I got her voicemail.

"Hey Mariah, it's Zac. I really need to talk to you. Call me back when you get this." I felt terrible. There was a bruise forming on my tailbone from where I'd hit the ground, and the ache in my arm seemed to be ever-present those days. Laying on my stomach in bed, I fell asleep. I woke to my cell phone vibrating on my side table about half an hour later.

"Hello?" I answered groggily.

"Hey, Zac. I just got home." It was Mariah. I snapped into focus and remembered why I needed to talk to her.

"Can you meet me somewhere, now, please?" I asked.

"Yeah, sure. Where?" She sounded worried.

"Meet me halfway between our houses, at the field." I didn't want to go back to the park.

"Yeah, okay. I'll see you soon." We hung up and I hurried downstairs and out the front door. I got to the field before Mariah, but she arrived shortly after.

"Hey, Zac. What's wrong?" She walked over and sat next to me, pulling her knees up to her chest.

"Remember how you said I can tell you anything?" I held my breath and stared at the ground.

"Yeah, anything. What is it?" She put her hand on my arm, and I let out my breath.

"I don't know how to explain this, but I'll try. Ever since the night Alana died, I've been having these flashbacks. They are mostly good memories, or flashes of us having fun at the park that night. But there is this one, it's a girl yelling, I'm not sure who. I know it's not Alana though." Mariah inhaled sharply, but I continued. "I've heard it three times. Twice at the skate park, both times I fell, and once at the park, and I fell off the stupid seesaw. I can't take it anymore." I dug my hands into my hair and put my head on my knees. "I need to know what happened to her or else I'm worried this will keep happening." I shook uncontrollably, and my head pounded.

"Is there anything else you remember?" Mariah questioned, but I shook my head, and she sighed. "That explains a lot. I really wish I could help you. I hate seeing you like this. You haven't remembered anything else from that night though, right?" she asked. "Maybe you should stay away from heights. For the time being." Mariah shrugged and smirked.

"Yeah." I laughed. "That'll be real fun. Thanks anyway though. It's nice to have finally told someone."

"Well, how was your afternoon with Adriane?" Mariah asked, trying to lighten the mood.

"It was good at first. Her birthday is on Friday, and I think we're going to dinner sometime this weekend. I'm not sure now though."

"Why?" Mariah asked.

"Well, we were on the see-saw, and that was when I heard that yelling and fell. Then I kind of flipped out a bit. I think she thought she did something wrong. I told her she didn't, but she couldn't see what was going on in my head." I groaned. "She's *lucky* for that. My head is a bit messed up at the moment."

"I wouldn't worry too much over it. You can smooth it over tomorrow. If she doesn't accept that you have some things going on in your life that you can't talk about, then maybe she's not worth the trouble." She paused for a second and added, "Also, I told you so." Mariah laughed and pushed me over.

"What are you talking about?" I rubbed my arm.

"I told you that you liked her." She giggled.

"Whatever," I mumbled, unable to hide my grin. "Thanks again, for everything."

"No problem. I can help you out with any trouble's you may have with Adriane later, too," she teased.

"Oh, thanks," I said sarcastically. "I'm going to need your expertise." I shook my head. "I find it hard to remember anything about her."

"Adriane?" Mariah asked, confused.

"No. Ally. She had a distinct laugh and smile." I closed my eyes trying to picture Ally and reopened them when I came up with nothing. "I can't remember them. They disappeared along with her."

"Oh." Mariah let out a long breath. "She had that hair flip thing down too. I don't remember how she did it. It always made me laugh though." A tear slid down her cheek. "It feels as if she never existed," Mariah whispered.

"I know that she was here, though and that's all that matters. She was my best friend until Jake came along, and she was as real as Adriane is to me now." The sun had begun to dip down past the trees. I stood up. "I should be getting home."

"Me too. I'll see you tomorrow."

I didn't see Adriane the next day and it went by slowly, as usual. But I was able to search for one of the locations I'd pinpointed on my map. It was a smaller wooded area, and it only took about twenty minutes to walk the whole thing. I didn't find anything that I thought I'd find if Ally was buried there. No freshly turned dirt or tamped down path. But at least I could cross that place off my list.

On Friday I went looking for Adriane during my third period study hall. I'd gotten her flowers for her birthday, and to apologize about how horribly our day had ended at the park.

I found her in the library and walked up behind her, putting my hand on her shoulder. She jumped and turned around.

"Jeez, you scared me." She pulled her earbuds out of her ears.

"Sorry. I brought you these." I gave her the flowers from behind my back. "Happy birthday, Adriane."

She smiled, then stood up and hugged me. "Thank you."

"You're welcome and I'm also sorry about how things ended the other day. It had nothing to do with you. I haven't really been myself lately. Are we still going to dinner this weekend?" I asked hopefully.

"It's okay, I understand. But I would love to go out to dinner with you. When would you like to go?" she asked.

"Tonight?" I suggested, and she nodded, grinning. "I'll pick you up at seven.

She took my hand and sat back down. "What class are you in?" she asked.

"Study hall."

"You should stay down here with me." Her green eyes sparkled in the light.

"Okay," I agreed, trying to disguise my eagerness.

After school, I spent my time preparing for my date with Adriane, although I itched to search the next location on my list for Ally.

I decided to call Mariah for help with planning my date.

"Mariah, help me. I don't know where to take Adriane for dinner tonight," I pleaded with her.

"I knew you'd need my expertise," she said smugly. "You don't want to take her anywhere too expensive, because she'll think you're trying too hard, and you can't afford it." She laughed. "But you don't want to take her anywhere too cheap, because she'll think you don't care enough to take her someplace nicer."

"This is too hard," I groaned. Maybe there was a reason I'd never been in a relationship before. There was too much planning and forethought that needed to be done, and I didn't have the energy for that.

"I know. Anyway, do you know of any place that fits my guidelines?" Mariah asked.

"Not a clue. I never go out to eat. Unless it's like fast food or something." I was beginning to worry whether I'd be ready in time for my date, it was almost six o'clock.

"Well, we can work with this. I have an idea. You only have an hour, so I will come over to help you. You don't have to go anywhere, because you can have a picnic! See, even though you aren't spending that much money, it's sweet and thoughtful."

"Whatever, get over here!"

We hung up and I went downstairs to wait.

When Mariah arrived, she stepped inside casually, displaying the basket she had brought.

"I have the basket and I know you have a blanket. All we need is the food!" She skipped into the kitchen. "What does she like to eat?"

"I have no idea. She's been here once, and we had turkey sandwiches with soda." I began to panic.

"We can work with that, I guess. We'll make them subs instead. Do you have any sparkling cider?" she asked, rifling through the fridge.

"What?"

"Never mind. Come help me make these sandwiches."

I made the sandwiches while Mariah found a couple of sodas in the fridge. She put grapes and strawberries in the basket as well. "Do you have her birthday cake?"

"Aw man. I forgot. I'll get her a card and a cake or something on the way to pick her up."

"Okay. That's good. I'll work on making your backyard pretty while you go get that stuff and pick her up," Mariah offered.

"Works for me. I should go, I guess. Thanks for all your help."

I stopped on my way to Adriane's house and picked up the cake and card.

When I rang her doorbell, Officer Monroe opened the door. He checked for Adriane then turned back to me.

"This is only going to be a one-time thing, kid." He crossed his arms.

"What are you talking about?" I furrowed my brow, and then it clicked. *He thinks I killed Ally.*

"I don't want my daughter hanging around with you and your friends. You probably haven't even told her yet about what happened to your friend. I'm not saying I think you're guilty, but I will not allow my daughter to hang around with someone who is a suspect in my investigation. You understand me?"

"Yes, I do, and I understand why you would be concerned. But I will not stop hanging out with your daughter because you think I killed someone, when I *know* I didn't," I said, anger simmering in my veins. Footsteps on the stairs inside alerted us to Adriane's descent and we both turned our focus to her.

I smiled as she descended the stairs in a navy blue, strapless, knee-length dress. She wore a short, black unbuttoned sweater over it, and white converse, with her wavy hair loose. She looked perfect for our first date. She came and stood next to me.

"Bye, dad." She ushered him away from the door.

"You'll have her home by ten," Officer Monroe bluntly stated.

"Yes, sir," I responded. Adriane followed me out to my truck where I opened her door for her and drove us back to my house.

"Why are we going to your house?" Adriane asked.

"I decided we should have a picnic." I blushed.

"That's so sweet." Adriane grinned.

"Well, Mariah did most of the work, but I helped a little." I smiled playfully, hoping she wouldn't mind that Mariah had helped me with our date.

"Still sweet," Adriane reassured me.

Mariah had found some Christmas lights and hung them up on the porch in my backyard. A picnic blanket was placed on a table in the middle of the yard. Mariah was finishing setting up the food when we came around.

"I was hoping to leave before you got back." Mariah hurried over.

"It's okay. Adriane, if you don't mind waiting here a moment, I have to get some things out of my truck," I told her, and she nodded.

"That's fine."

I walked with Mariah to the front of my house.

"Thank you so much. I'm clueless when it comes to this stuff." I hugged her goodbye.

"No problem." She shrugged.

I sighed. "Adriane's dad hates me."

"What? Why?" Mariah asked.

"Remember, he's Officer Monroe, so he knows everything about the whole Ally thing, and he knows I'm a suspect," I explained.

"Oh." Mariah glanced around, "The less people who know about it the better. I have to go. Have fun." Mariah waved, then got into her car and drove away.

I grabbed the card and cake from my truck. Taking a deep breath, I went back around the house to where Adriane waited.

"Sorry I took so long," I apologized.

"No problem. Let's eat." Adriane sat down at the table. "You know, no one has ever done anything like this for me before."

"I'm glad you like it. I was having no luck thinking of any good dinner ideas on my own," I admitted.

"Well, this is perfect." Adriane grinned.

Once we finished eating, I cut the cake and gave her the card. We spent a while talking about random things, and I felt like *maybe* I could tell her about my status as a suspect in a missing person's investigation.

"Are you close with your dad?" I asked, trying not to seem too eager for her answer.

Adriane scrunched her nose. "Kind of. I'm much closer with my mom, but I still feel pretty close with my dad, I guess. What about you? Are you close with your parents?"

"Yeah, both of them. They've been helping me a lot with some things that have been going on recently." I remained vague to see if she would take the bait and let me know if she knew about Ally's case.

"That's nice," she said, not prying. I respected her for that, but also cursed inwardly. This was going to be harder than I thought. "Speaking of being close with people, you're friends with Josh, right?"

I tilted my head and nodded. "Yeah, why?"

"He got in a fight at school today, in the hall. I could see some of it from the upper atrium before the teachers were able to break it up."

Again? I thought. He'd been getting into a lot of fights lately.

"That's weird," I said, but when I thought about it, it wasn't all that weird. The few fights that I'd witnessed throughout school had usually featured Josh. But he wasn't always the one to start it. "He has a bit of a temper sometimes." I needed to get us back on the topic of our parents so I could see if her dad told her anything about Ally.

Before I could ask another vaguely leading question, she said, "Tonight was great, thank you so much, for everything." A blush tinted her cheeks as she smiled.

"You're welcome. But there is something I need to tell you..." I trailed off, thinking about how I could explain that I was a suspect in Ally's case to her without scaring her off.

"What is it?" she asked.

I chickened out and decided to wait a little bit longer.

"You look amazing tonight," I told her instead.

"I'm glad you think so, I was worried I would be overdressed." She leaned closer, but I pulled back quickly as I noticed the time on my phone. It was nearly nine forty-five and I had to have her home before ten or else I risked giving Officer Monroe one more thing to hold against me.

"Come on, I should get you home." We stood from the table and walked out to the car.

"What are you doing tomorrow?" Adriane asked.

"Well actually, I was going to ask if you wanted to come to a Halloween party with me. It's at my friend Aaron's house." I'd completely forgotten about it until that moment. It seemed like it had been much longer than a few days since I'd last hung out with my friends.

"Oh, yeah, sure. That would be fun." She smiled. "Should I dress up? Or is it a no-costume kind of Halloween party?"

"I mean, I don't plan on dressing up, but I'm pretty sure everyone else is, so either way is fine by me."

Adriane nodded and appeared thoughtful, her brow crinkling as she pursed her lips. "I'll try to come up with something."

"Perfect. I'll pick you up around eight?" I offered and then realized that was probably a bad idea since her dad hated me. "Or I can have Mariah pick you up."

"That would probably be better. I highly doubt my dad would be okay with me going to a Halloween party with you. Not because he doesn't like you, but because you're a guy. And he's a little overprotective." She twisted a lock of her hair.

"I get it, don't worry. Mariah will pick you up and bring you to my house. But for now, let's get you home so your dad might let you leave again."

She grinned.

Once we were at her house, I walked her to the door and of course, Officer Monroe opened it once we reached the top step of the porch.

"Well, I'll see you later," I said awkwardly.

Adriane mouthed, *sorry,* and said, "Thank you. I had fun." She bounced inside and went up the stairs.

"Goodnight, sir," I said, turning away from Officer Monroe. He said nothing, but the door shut a little too forcefully for me not to take notice.

In the morning, Mom made breakfast but had to get back to work before I woke up. I used my free time to check the next location on my list for Ally. It was a larger area than the first place, but further from the park. I couldn't imagine that whoever had moved her body had wanted to take the time traveling too far in case they were caught.

To no surprise, I found nothing there.

On my drive home, I called Mariah.

"I told Adriane you would pick her up at eight tonight for the party. I hope that's okay. I didn't want to deal with her dad," I explained, hoping she wouldn't mind that I'd offered without asking.

"That's fine. Am I picking you up after?" she asked.

"Well, Jess and Katrina are bringing the van so we can all cram in and ride over together." Katrina didn't always hang out with our group, so I figured it would make tonight the perfect opportunity to ask her about what she remembered from the night Ally disappeared.

"That sounds good. What are you going as tonight?" Mariah cut through my thoughts.

"Uh, myself," I laughed. "I don't dress up."

Mariah groaned. "Oh, come on, that is so lame."

"What are you going as, then?"

"I'm going to be Little Red Riding Hood. I get to wear a hooded cape, and it's awesome." We both laughed. "But you *need* to dress up. You could be like a lumberjack or something. You've already got all you need for that."

"What are you trying to say?"

"That you are a Mainer, through and through," Mariah joked. "If I get to your house later, and you are not dressed up, prepare for my wrath. Muah ha ha."

I couldn't help but think of Ally and how she always used to tease me like that. Mariah and she were so much alike. I pushed those thoughts away.

"All right, all right. I'll do the stupid lumberjack thing. I think my dad has some suspenders I can borrow, and I've got the rest," I caved.

"Perfect! Well, I have to go, but I'll see you tonight!" Mariah hung up.

When I got home, I found my dad's suspenders, a beanie, one of my many flannels, and a pair of worn jeans. Mariah was right, and it was easy to put together.

That night, I pulled on my work boots with my outfit, and I was ready to go. It didn't really feel all that different from what I wore every day, and I wasn't sure if I should be ashamed of that or not.

There was a knock on the door, and I strolled over to open it. Josh leaned against the doorframe in his Thor costume, swinging his hammer casually.

"Nice costume," he said, smirking.

"It was easy and didn't cost me anything," I justified.

"This one cost me a fortune, but all the ladies love it." We both laughed at that. My jaw dropped when I saw Michael outside waiting in the van. He wore a banana costume and took up the whole middle section of the van.

"Seriously? You didn't even try, dude," he said, looking me up and down. "You'll have to sit in the slacker section." He nodded to the back seat of the van.

"Hey! We are not slackers!" Katrina protested, smirking. She and Jess sat in the back seat dressed as Mario and Luigi, but in much less clothing than the actual Mario and Luigi would wear.

"They tried harder than I did," I said, and Michael nodded, saying "true." Mariah and Adriane pulled into the driveway.

"Sorry we're late!" Mariah said as she stepped out of her car. "Her dad had a lot of questions about what we were doing tonight. We almost didn't make it out alive."

"Sorry." Adriane glanced sheepishly at the ground. "I couldn't exactly tell him the truth."

"It's all good, we just got here anyway," Josh said, waving his hand. Mariah avoided Josh, going to her trunk to retrieve her cape. She took off her sweatpants and sweatshirt, revealing her actual costume. It was much like Jess and Katrina's costumes: short shorts, with a corset top.

"Don't worry, Adriane has her costume too." Mariah smirked, giving me a wink. "I would not have let her come otherwise." Adriane pulled off her sweatpants and sweatshirt as well, revealing her Lara Croft costume. Mariah handed her the gun holster from her trunk.

"I had to braid her hair before we came, which was another reason we were running late." Mariah flipped Adriane's braid up over her shoulder.

"You look great," I said, and Adriane did a twirl, showing off her costume.

"Let's get going, gang," Jess called from the driver's seat. Zac figured she was the DD for the night. Josh got into the driver's seat, and Mariah took the passenger seat, to my surprise. I figured she'd sit in the back to be as far from Josh as possible.

"Are you all right sitting on Zac's lap, Adriane?" Michael asked, with a hint of teasing in his voice. There should have been enough seats in the van, but Michael's costume took up way too much room.

"Uh, yeah. Of course." Her cheeks turned a little red, but she climbed into the van after me.

"If you're uncomfortable, I can sit on Michael's lap," I offered, half-joking.

"No, I'm good," she said, sitting on my lap without hesitation.

Michael shut the door, and we were off. Adriane leaned back against my chest, and I put my good arm around her to keep her from lurching forward every time we stopped.

"I don't understand how you girls do it, I would be freezing in those shorts," Michael commented. Katrina stretched her legs up, propping them on the back of the middle seat.

"We're going to be inside the whole time anyway. I don't know how *you* do it. Aren't you sweating in that thing?" Katrina swatted at the stem of the banana costume that extended toward her.

"Touché." Michael laughed, and deliberately stretched out to take up even more space in the van.

"You are ridiculous," Katrina teased, pushing his costume back into his own space. I could feel Adriane laughing.

"You wish you could look as good as us in these outfits," Mariah chimed in. Katrina and Jess gave their assenting "Yups."

"Next year, I'm going to prove I *can* look as good in one of those outfits," Michael declared.

"I say we hold him to that," I added.

"Oh, we for sure will," Jess said.

"What, you don't trust that I'll actually do it? I would do it right now if I had the outfit handy."

I didn't doubt that he would. Michael was always doing things for the laughs, and he was better at it than the rest of our group.

"We'll settle for next Halloween," Jess said. "It will be our last Halloween together before college, so it will be sure to make it memorable."

We pulled into Aaron's long dirt driveway, which was off the beaten path. He had no neighbors, so it was the perfect spot for a party. We spilled out of the van.

"Wow," Adriane gaped at the house as we entered it. Aaron's house was practically a mansion. It had three floors, and the entryway was as big as my whole first floor.

"I know. I have no idea what his parents do for a living, but whatever it is, I'm in," I joked.

Hanging from the ceiling of the entryway, which was about fifty feet high, was an extremely expensive-looking crystal chandelier. The crystals vibrated in time with the bass coming from the speakers.

After the entryway, there was the game room. It had air hockey, foosball, a giant flat screen to play all the gaming systems on, and a Ping-Pong table where beer pong was being set up. There was also a little sitting area in the middle of the room with two three-person couches facing each other. A fully stocked bar sat in the back corner of the game room where Aaron stood handing out drinks, and beside him were the kegs. It seemed almost impossible that his parents wouldn't notice the missing food and drinks when they got home, but Aaron always managed to restock everything before they noticed anything amiss.

"Do you want a drink?" I offered Adriane, and she nodded. "What would you like? Aaron makes pretty good mixed drinks, or there's beer and soda."

"We can check out the mixed drinks, I'm not really a fan of beer." She shrugged. I led her over to the bar where Aaron was mixing the drinks.

"Hey, Zac! How's it going?" Aaron looked up briefly from the bar.

"Hey, not too bad. Have you met Adriane?" I put my arm around her waist, pulling her closer to my side.

"Yeah, I think we have a class or two together. What would you like to drink? I've got vodka, rum, tequila, and whiskey," he offered.

"Rum and coke?" Adriane said it like a question, and Aaron nodded, pulling out the Bacardi and a liter of Coke. He poured the two into a red solo cup and passed it to Adriane.

"Thanks."

"And for Zac..." Aaron pulled out a can of Busch beer and slid it over to me. "Same as always."

"Of course. Thanks, man." I popped the top on the can and took a sip.

"Zac!" I turned to see who was calling me and saw Josh walking toward me. "You up for a game of pong?"

"I don't know." I turned to Adriane. "Do you want to play?"

Her eyes widened. "I mean, I've never played before, I may not be any good." She blushed.

"Not a problem. You can be on my team, I'll carry us," Josh said, looping his arm through hers and leading her away.

"You're going to let him steal your girl that easily?" Aaron stepped out from behind the bar and smirked. "I need a break; I'll be Josh's partner." I nodded in thanks and headed to the pong table. There were ten cups forming a triangle on each side of the table. Josh was already showing Adriane the basics of the game, and she was laughing at some stupid joke he had probably told.

"Hope you don't mind if I steal your partner." I stepped up beside Adriane and placed my hand on the small of her back, which her crop top left bare. She gave me a grateful look and smiled.

"I thought she should learn from the best." Josh shrugged, feigning innocence.

"And she will." I smirked and led Adriane to the other side of the table. Aaron joined Josh on his side.

"It's really simple, throw the ball into one of their cups," I explained. "Stand here." I placed my hands on her hips and guided her to the proper distance from the table and let her lean back against me as she took her aim. Her first try landed directly in the center cup.

"Perfect," I murmured, and she turned to look up at me, grinning. Josh followed her lead and sank his ball into the middle cup on our side.

"Don't forget the most important rule," Josh called to us. I rolled my eyes.

"Whenever someone gets a ball in, the other team has to drink. So, we usually take turns drinking, but if you want me to do it every time, I can," I offered.

"We can take turns. Ladies first?" she asked with a wink.

"Of course. Your choice, a couple sip of your own drink, or half a shot."

"Umm, half a shot I guess." Adriane took a shot glass from the table and the vodka set there for the pong games and poured herself half a shot. "No chasers over here I assume?" She cocked an eyebrow, but took the shot before I could answer, and chased it with her rum and coke.

"Onward!" Josh called out.

I stepped up to the table and took aim.

The game went on for half an hour, and finally Adriane sank the last shot. She'd had to drink two full shots, and I had to chug one and a half beers.

"For your first time, you did a pretty great job," I said, and Adriane smirked.

"All right, who wants to take on the winners!" Josh called out to the couple of people standing around in the living room.

"We have to play again?" Adriane raised her eyebrows, and I could tell she needed a break. I did too.

"No, not at all. We can do whatever you want." I waved Josh over. "You and Aaron can take on the next team; Adriane and I are going to sit this one out."

"Perfect. Clearly I need to practice so I can beat you guys next time," Josh said, clapping me on the shoulder.

I led Adriane away from the pong table, and toward the kitchen. We bumped into Jess and Michael on our way.

"Oh. My. God," I said. Adriane and I burst out laughing. Jess and Michael had swapped costumes.

"It was a bet, man. You know I can't turn down a bet." Michael shrugged, his cropped top scrunching up even more.

"But at what cost for the rest of us?" I could barely contain my laughter.

"But I was right, I look as good as Jess in this costume." Michael smirked and struck a pose.

"You look all right." Jess shrugged, but she laughed too.

A laugh that was all too familiar came from behind me. I whipped around, but there was no one there. I had heard Ally's laugh. As I turned back around, the others all looked at me a little confused.

"Is everything all right?" Adriane put her hand on my arm, and concern creased her brow. I shook my head trying to clear it and figured it must have been the alcohol messing with me.

"Yeah, fine. Sorry, I thought I heard something." I tried to smile. "I need another drink." Making my way back to the bar, I grabbed another beer. Adriane hung back with Jess and Michael, talking about something I couldn't hear. I stayed by the bar for a moment as a dizzy spell came over me. Bracing myself on the bar, I squeezed my eyes shut as the whole world shifted around me. I heard Ally's laugh again.

"Hahaha! I win again!" she said. Her voice echoed in my mind, but otherwise, there was blackness. *"Give me a reason to stay up here..."* Then the voice changed, *"Who invited you?"* That was Jake's voice. And the scream he still couldn't pinpoint.

I gasped and opened my eyes, releasing my death grip on the bar. I squeezed my head, trying to extract the memories that were so close, but out of reach. That scream... It *could* have been Ally. It was more frantic and higher pitched than I was used to.

"Zac, is everything all right?" Katrina's voice broke through the fog that had formed in my mind.

"Yeah, some memories," I told her, and she nodded in understanding, but she still looked worried. "Sorry, I don't mean to be a downer, but what do *you* remember from the night Ally disappeared?"

Katrina's eyes widened and she tucked her hair behind her ear. "I mean I didn't lose any memories like you. I remember being at the park, and hanging out with everyone, but then Joe and I left."

I nodded. That was pretty much everyone's story. *I didn't see anything. I left. I wasn't there.*

"Well, thanks anyway. I feel like I'm going crazy," I admitted. It was not *normal* to hear voices.

"This may not help, but maybe it will." Katrina placed two shot glasses on top of the bar, grabbed a bottle of Bacardi from beneath the bar, and poured it. "Do a shot with me." She smirked. I laughed but picked up one of the glasses.

"Fine. But if this makes me even more crazy, *you* will be responsible for reeling me back in."

Katrina lifted her shot glass and clinked it with mine.

"Fair enough." She nodded and we both downed our shots, making equally repulsed faces after and laughing at each other. "Disgusting." She shook her head like she was trying to shake away the burn of the shot.

"We're feeling left out," Jess said, as she, Michael, and Adriane walked over to join us at the bar. Katrina clasped her hand over her mouth, on the verge of bursting out in laughter at the sight of Michael in Jess's costume.

"I think I will *need* another shot to try to get this image out of my mind," Katrina joked, grabbing three more shot glasses from under the bar.

"I find that insulting." Michael feigned being hurt, but he could not hold back his own laughter. Katrina poured the five shots.

"Ooh shots! Count me in!" Mariah skipped over to us.

"Here, take this one," Jess said, placing a shot in front of Mariah. "I'm driving."

"Anyone else, before I hang up my bartender hat?" Katrina glanced around. "Good. Let's get this over with." Everyone grabbed a shot glass, and on the count of three, or two for the overeager ones, we all threw back our shots.

"Even worse the second time," I gasped, as Mariah sputtered.

"Blech." Mariah grabbed a bottle of Coke and filled her shot glass with it, chasing the rum.

"It's not so bad!" Michael laughed, and Jess rolled her eyes.

"That's my signal that you need a break. Come on, let's go get you some water." Jess took Michael's hand and led him away toward the kitchen. Katrina followed them, and Mariah was dragged into a game of pong by Aaron, leaving me alone with Adriane.

"So, is everything okay?" Adriane turned to me. There was worry and possibly some jealousy in her expression.

"Everything's great, why?" I asked, confused.

"Well, I saw you over here before and you looked like you were in pain, and I was going to come over, but Katrina showed up, and I didn't want to interrupt anything." Her cheeks flushed pink as she turned her gaze to the floor.

"Oh no, Katrina and I, there is nothing between us, don't worry about that," I told her, giving her a reassuring smile, which seemed to ease her mind a bit. "As for me, my arm was bothering me a bit," I lied, not ready to admit to what was *really* going on in my head.

"Oh, okay. Now I feel a little stupid." She laughed, and I took her hand.

"Don't feel stupid. You can ask me about anything." I felt dishonest saying it, since I was withholding so much from her.

"All right," she smirked. "I like your friends. They seem fun."

"Oh, they're definitely something. This is the tip of the iceberg, the ride home will be a shit show, and you may rethink your assessment of them."

Adriane laughed.

We spent the rest of the night enjoying each other's company and talking about random topics, made even more interesting by the buzz we both had from the alcohol. Occasionally, Michael or Katrina, or one of the others would come to hang out for a bit, but they always continued on their way, leaving Adriane and I to ourselves.

At the end of the night, we had both mostly sobered up and oversaw rounding up all the others. Michael had passed out on one of the couches, back in his banana costume, and Mariah, who sat beside him, was too wobbly to help him out to the car. Josh and I had to half drag him to the car.

"He couldn't have kept the Luigi costume on? It would have been so much easier to maneuver him," Josh said through gritted teeth. Michael was tall and built *without* the banana costume. He woke up enough to climb into the van, but I had to squish the rest of his costume in with him.

Adriane helped Jess with Katrina, who was almost as far gone as Michael, but at least she was still awake, and Mariah was drunk, but not so much that she couldn't get herself to the car. Jess hopped into the driver's seat.

"All right, do we have everyone?" she asked, looking back in the rear-view mirror.

"Everyone is present and accounted for," Mariah teased. "Though, I could argue that Michael is not actually *present*."

Jess was satisfied with that answer, so she started the car. Adriane leaned heavily against me as we drove down the road, and I realized she'd fallen asleep. I gripped her a little tighter, to make sure she wouldn't fall, not that there was much room to move anywhere.

Once we reached my house, everyone piled out of the car, except for Michael, who was still asleep.

"Is everyone staying here tonight?" I asked, yawning.

"Yepperooni." Katrina grinned, and stumbled, even though she was standing still. Jess stepped up and helped Katrina inside, followed by Josh supporting Michael, who was mostly awake.

"If either of you want to go home, I can bring you," Jess offered to Mariah and Adriane after she'd delivered Katrina safely inside.

"I told my parents I was sleeping over at Mariah's." Adriane shrugged. "So, it's up to her."

"If you don't mind bringing us to my house, that would be great. I promised my mom I'd be home tonight," Mariah said, and Jess nodded.

"Yeah, come on," Jess got back into the van.

"I'll come get my car in the morning," Mariah said as she hugged me goodbye. "See you tomorrow."

"Text me when you get home," I said, and turned to Adriane. I wasn't sure if I should hug her, kiss her, or neither. She stepped up to me and kissed my cheek, solving my inner dilemma.

"I'll see you later," she said as she turned back, giving me a small wave. I smiled and waved as they drove away.

Chapter Ten
Alana
Eight days before

I drove Clyde's car home and Clyde was still lounging on the couch when I walked inside. "How was your dinner?" he asked casually.

"It sucked, as usual, but you probably already knew that." I sighed, sinking onto the couch. I truly had no desire to be near Clyde, but I had to talk about this with someone, and he was there.

"Yeah, those dinners usually end badly. What did Jake say this time?" Clyde asked, sounding like he cared for once.

"Same old same old. That loving him changes nothing and that I needed to get the hell out of his house. Lovely times." I laughed despite everything that had happened.

"Sounds like you need to find a new boyfriend," Clyde said.

I wasn't sure if I should agree with that, considering Clyde wasn't exactly a prime example of a good boyfriend.

"Or you can stay with him, and torture that friend Zac of yours a little more."

"You have no right to say that!" I yelled, infuriated. "You know nothing about my relationship with Zac, or Jake for that matter!" I jumped off the couch and ran upstairs. I couldn't believe I'd allowed Clyde to get to me. He was always trying to push my buttons. I slammed my bedroom door and threw myself onto my bed. The phone rang, and I already knew who it was. I picked it up.

"STOP CALLING!" I yelled and slammed down the receiver. Running downstairs, I went out the front door. It was getting dark out, but I could see Zac standing in his driveway with Aaron. I walked over to them, and they watched me curiously, until I shoved Zac and he nearly fell to the ground.

"What the hell?" Aaron yelled.

"This has nothing to do with you," I snapped, and turned back to Zac. "Why did you have to tell me you loved me? Everything was fine until then! We were happy. I was happy." I let out all my anger on him.

"What are you talking about?" Zac remained calm, which pissed me off even more.

"Don't act like you don't remember!" I hoped that he hadn't forgotten all about me.

"That was like a year ago." Zac shrugged.

"If it seems so long ago to you now, why can't we still be friends?" All my anger left me in a rush and was replaced with grief. The grief that I had never truly felt over our lost friendship. Tears spilled down my cheeks and I had to turn away from Zac. I walked briskly back down the driveway toward my house.

Zac caught up with me and grabbed my hand. "Look, I'm sorry. I still care about you. We were best friends, Ally, and we can go back to being friends if that's what you want. It's hard for me to watch you with Jake. I don't want Jake hurting you, and if he ever did, I don't know what I would do. Probably kick his ass or something." Zac smirked.

"You don't want to see me hurt? Zac, you were the one who hurt me! I lost you as my best friend at a moment when I probably needed you most!" Zac seemed at a loss for words, so I continued. "I want us to be friends again, I do. I don't know if it's that simple."

"Ally," Zac grinned. "It's always simple with us. Let's hang out like we used to. We can have an Uno night." Zac took a step toward me, but I backed away.

"All right. Text me when you're free and I'll come over. I should probably go now that I've embarrassed myself thoroughly. See you later." I turned and walked back to my house, wiping away the tears.

Before bed that night, I tried calling Jake, but he didn't answer. I waited a while to see if he called back and ended up falling asleep. In the morning, I woke to a knock on my door.

"Whosit?" I mumbled, trying to wake up.

"Your boy is here," Clyde grumbled through the door.

"Jake's here? What time is it?" I looked at the clock. It was nearly noon. I rolled over onto my stomach, and a few minutes later, Jake was stomping up the stairs into my room.

"Ally, wake up. I need to talk to you." Jake sat on the edge of my bed. I attempted to push him off, but my arms were like noodles after waking up.

"Go away," I mumbled.

"Come on, don't be like that. I just want to talk." Jake put his hand on my arm, but I pulled it away. "Ally..."

"Jakey," I mocked. "Leave me alone." I put my pillow over my head, hoping he would take the hint.

"I'm sorry about last night. I shouldn't have yelled at you," he tried to apologize, but I was in no mood to accept his apology.

"You're right. You shouldn't have, but you did. Now, as you might say, get the hell out of my house." I could only hope that it would hurt him as much as it hurt me, but I doubted it.

"I wish you wouldn't be like this, but I guess I'll go." He turned to leave, and I finally sat up. Looking hopeful that I was coming around, Jake paused, watching me.

"I think I want to take a break. I don't want you to call me or text me until I'm ready to talk," I said bluntly. When this registered in Jake's mind, he gaped at me for a moment, and turned on his heel, storming out.

I collapsed back onto my bed and realized what I had done. I broke up with Jake.

Covering my face with my blanket, I tried to fight back tears. *What have I done?* I'd hurt one of the people that I loved most in the world.

I wasn't sure if I wanted to take back what I'd done, but I knew that it would feel better to have Jake there with me. I reached for my phone, but it fell onto the floor.

There was nothing I could do but cry. Why couldn't I have thought it through first? I loved Jake, why did I need a break? I didn't need one. I would give it a little time, then I would call him, and everything would be fine.

I stayed in bed all day, realizing little by little that maybe I *didn't* want Jake back. There was always that small part of me that was yearning for him, but there was a large part of me that knew I could do so much better. There was someone out there who would love me and treat me better than Jake ever did. Yet, I still loved him and every time I fell asleep, I dreamt of him.

At the end of the day, I made my decision. I didn't call Jake. I figured our relationship was something better discussed in person. I would talk to him at school in the morning if he bothered to show up.

Chapter Eleven
Zac

The next morning, Mariah and Adriane walked over to pick up Mariah's car before anyone was even awake in my house.

After everyone else left, I decided to check another location off my checklist in my search for Ally. This time, I could tell right away it wouldn't be where she was found. Since the map had been made that depicted it as a wooded area, most of the trees had been taken down to start developing new homes.

Sinking down onto the sidewalk, I put my head in my hands. "I need you, Ally. I need you now more than ever. I need you to help me with this whole thing with Adriane, and I need you to help me with the flashbacks that are haunting me. I need you to help me deal with losing you. I'm falling to pieces." I allowed myself to cry the tears that I'd been holding back. I hyperventilated, barely able to breathe. The cold air made my throat raw, so I decided to go back to my truck.

I'd finally reached my breaking point. The point where it all hit me. Where reality finally caught up with me and I couldn't pretend as if Ally were coming back anymore. I couldn't drive because I could barely see through my tears. Everything was blurry and I was overcome with exhaustion. I reclined my seat and closed my eyes.

I woke up an hour later with a pain in my neck and my broken arm throbbing. Looking in the mirror, I realized I looked terrible. My eyes were puffy, and my hair stuck out in all directions. I started my truck and drove home.

When I got home, Mom was in the living room watching TV.

"Hey sweetie, you left your phone on the counter. Mariah and Adriane both called asking where you were," she said.

"Thanks. I'll call them back," I muttered.

"I was calling to say hi, is that lame?" Adriane said when I called her. I forced a laugh.

"Oh, no that's not lame," I said, stifling a yawn.

"Good. So, what's going on?" she asked.

"Nothing. I don't feel so great. I think I'm going to bed. I'll talk to you tomorrow." Another fresh wave of grief threatened to pull me back into the darkness.

"Oh, okay." She sounded worried but didn't press me. "Well, I hope you feel better." She hung up.

I lay in bed and tried to fall asleep. Once I finally did, it wasn't much better than being awake. Nightmares of Ally's death haunted me. Unfortunately, there wasn't even anything helpful in my nightmares. No recalled memories or leads.

When I woke, my room was too bright. I hadn't closed my blinds and the sun streamed through my window, lighting up every nook.

I cursed as I realized I'd slept in. First period would end shortly at school, and I couldn't have any more absences.

Groaning, I moved to get out of bed, my foot snagging on my comforter and dragging it with me. I threw on my usual attire, which was pretty much what I'd worn to the Halloween part, minus the suspenders.

As I hurried out the door, I checked my phone for the first time. There was a text from Adriane.

Want to hang out after school today?

I typed *definitely,* then backspaced, not wanting to sound too eager, and sending *sure,* instead.

When I got to school, I parked in the last row of the lot and strode in as the bell rang for the end of first period.

"Fashionably late." Mariah veered toward me, looping her arm around mine. "And looking like you never changed out of your costume," she teased, plucking at the sleeve of my flannel.

"Do anything fun yesterday?" I asked as we walked toward my next class.

Mariah grimaced, but replaced it with a smile quickly, as if I wasn't supposed to see that.

"Nothing terribly exciting. Adriane and I spent some time chatting after I dropped her off at her house, but then I went home and worked on homework. How about you?" She turned her smile on me.

It was the first time I noticed the bags under her eyes. The extreme exhaustion that seemed to be plaguing her, and shame washed over me. I'd been so wrapped up with my own grief and investigating that I hadn't noticed those around me were also suffering.

"How are you doing, Mariah?" I asked, lowering my voice so no one would listen in.

She looked taken aback. "I - uh, I'm fine," she said, blinking rapidly. Taking her arm from mine, she backed away. "I've got to get to class. I'll talk to you later."

After school, Adriane met me at my truck. To my surprise, Josh and Aaron were also there.

"What's going on?" I asked as I walked up to them, putting my arm around Adriane's shoulders.

"We're going riding at my house, you want in?" Aaron said, grinning.

I lifted my broken arm slightly and Aaron nodded in understanding.

"Right. I keep forgetting about that. Sucks." Aaron leaned back against the hood of my truck. "Adriane could drive for you," he suggested, lifting a brow at her.

Adriane's shoulders shook from laughter. "I don't even know what we're talking about, but I've never driven anything other than a car."

"Four-wheeler," I told her. "It's really easy. I could teach you, if you want."

"Maybe you shouldn't ride today," Josh said, his eye twitching. He seemed a little off today, but I couldn't pinpoint why. "Don't want to risk hurting yourself again."

Adriane leaned into me. "If you want to go, I'm happy to be your chauffeur," she teased. "I learn quickly."

"All right, guess we'll see you in a bit then," Aaron said, pushing off from my truck and heading for his own. "Come on, Joshua." Josh rolled his eyes. Aaron liked to torment him by using his full name. He did it to all of us from time to time.

Once we were in my truck, I asked Adriane, "You sure you really want to do this? It's totally fine if you don't want to hang out at Aaron's."

"I'm sure," she said, taking my hand. "Unless *you* don't want to. But I've always wanted to learn how to drive an ATV, now is the perfect time."

"All right."

We drove to Aaron's house from there.

A few years ago, we made a trail in the woods beside Aaron's house for four-wheeling and dirt biking. It was the perfect location for us, since there really weren't any good trails near our town.

When we got to Aaron's, everyone else was already there and Josh was in the middle of getting his dirt bike out of the shed we kept all our ATVs in.

"Hey, Zac!" Michael greeted me from the porch where he sat with Jess and Katrina.

"Hey!" I called back.

Aaron already had his dirt bike ready to go and Michael's four-wheeler idled beside the porch. Aaron helped me get my four-wheeler out of the shed, since I was down an arm.

"You sure you're going to be able to ride with a broken arm?" Michael asked Zac as he walked up behind me.

"I'm going to be a passenger princess today," I joked. "Adriane will be driving."

Aaron, Michael, and Josh put on their helmets and readied themselves. Jess ran out of the house and hopped onto the back of Michael's four-wheeler. I grabbed my helmet from the back of my four-wheeler and realized I didn't have an extra.

"Here." I held it out to Adriane. "My head is already screwed up; we can at least protect you."

She smiled but cocked her head as if she didn't entirely catch on to what I was saying, and I remembered I hadn't told her anything about Ally or the fact that I'd lost my memories of the night she'd disappeared. Thankfully she didn't question me, though, and took the helmet.

Holding my hand, I said, "You first."

Adriane stepped onto the four-wheeler, swinging her leg over it and settling in. I followed suit, sitting behind her and reaching my good arm to point to the levers and buttons on the handles of the ATV.

"This is the gas." I touched the lever on the inside of the right handle. "This is the front brakes." Moving my hand to the lever on the outside of the right handle, I pulled it.

"Okay," Adriane breathed, turning her head slightly so she could look at me. My chest was pressed against her back, and I noticed a flush creeping up her neck. I hadn't thought about how intimate this would be, but now that I had, my face heated and I bit my lip as I tried to hide my smile.

"What about this one?" she asked, pointing to the lever on the left handle.

"That is the back breaks," I said. "You can use both at the same time, but if you're going to do either, I'd chose the back over the front. Or else we may wind up flipping over."

"Got it." Adriane put her hands on the handles and took a deep breath. "Are we ready?"

I wrapped my good arm around her waist.

"I'm ready if you are."

Adriane pulled on the gas lever gently at first, making us move at a snail's pace. But once she seemed to become more comfortable, she increased our speed.

I hadn't ridden my four-wheeler since Ally died. It was nice to be riding again, and even better with Adriane. Riding alone would make me feel the absence of Ally more than I would like. Adriane's warm body pressed against mine kept me warm in the crisp November air. The wind whipped through my hair and made me feel like I was flying.

I thanked God that I wasn't driving when my vision narrowed, and my heart raced.

I could faintly hear Adriane.

"Zac? Are you all right?" she asked.

"Zac, are you all right? You just... Collapsed. I don't know what to do. Please, Zac..." I couldn't tell who was talking to me, but she was sobbing.

"Zac?"

We'd come to a stop. My grip on Adriane had tightened and she must have sensed something was off because she'd turned to look at me and worry lines creased her forehead.

I cleared my throat. "Yeah, I'm fine." The trail came back into view.

"Okay, let me know if you need me to stop again," she said.

Thankfully I had no more flashbacks or blackouts. We drove around on the trail until darkness fell. Then, we all went inside Aaron's house for dinner.

While I drove Adriane home, I decided to take a risk and ask her about the investigation into Ally's disappearance.

"So, your dad is a cop, right?" I asked, keeping my eyes on the road so I wouldn't seem too eager.

"Yeah, why?" Adriane didn't sound suspicious, so I went on.

"Just curious if he ever talks to you about any of his cases. Seems like he'd have a lot of good stories to tell."

She hummed to herself, as if considering her answer. "There's a lot he's not allowed to talk about, but sometimes he shares little pieces, or stories."

"Has he told you anything about recent cases? Or maybe the one he's currently working on?"

"You mean the one that has to do with the girl from our school who went missing?" she asked, suspicion tightening her voice. "I'm not supposed to talk about it with anyone."

"Yeah, of course." I shrugged and tried to play it off like I hadn't really cared anyway, but I was pretty sure I'd overstepped.

We pulled into her driveway, and she turned to me, her hand on the door handle.

"I have to work tomorrow, but do you want to pick me up and we can see a movie or something after?" she asked.

My shoulders relaxed with relief that I hadn't scared her off with my questions. "Sure. I'll see you then, unless I see you at school."

She leaned in and kissed me.

After I got out of the truck, my phone vibrated in my cup holder. I glanced down, and *Mom* was written across the screen.

I heard from your therapist that you told her I'd be making your next appointment. So, I did. Day after tomorrow, three o'clock.

I groaned in annoyance. There'd been a small part of me that thought I might get away with lying to them both, but I should have known they'd figure it out sooner or later. It wasn't like I *had* to go. If I told my mom that I didn't think it was helping, she'd probably let me off the hook, but it made her feel better knowing I was talking with someone about my supposed trauma. So, I'd go talk to the therapist one more time, and hopefully that would be enough for my mom to forget about it.

After school the next day, a deep sense of dread had made a ball in my stomach. I couldn't pinpoint what the cause was, but there was so much still going on, I chalked it up to Ally's case.

In an effort to soothe my nerves before going out with Adriane that night, I took a nap.

"Zac, do you want to come downstairs and eat dinner?" Mom called up the stairs, waking me.

Blinking slowly, I remembered where I was and what day it was. I grabbed my phone, checking the time. Adriane had texted.

I'm done at 7.

I swore as I realized it was almost that time. I hadn't expected to sleep so long. Jumping out of bed, I ran downstairs.

I called to Mom as I went, "I'm picking up Adriane at the skate park. Sorry, Mom." I rushed out the door.

"Yeah, sure," Mom responded.

Adriane waited outside for me as I pulled up five minutes late. She gave me a tight smile when she climbed into the passenger seat, and I knew something was wrong. Dread snowballed in my stomach.

"How was your day?" I asked, pulling out of the parking lot.

Adriane remained quiet for a few extra beats, and then she sighed and turned to me.

"Today was a little stressful. When I got home last night, my dad talked to me about something. It was kind of funny that you'd asked whether he told me about his cases, because that's exactly what he wanted to talk about."

My grip tightened on the wheel, and I slowed down to the speed limit as I tried not to jump to any conclusions about what her dad had told her.

"Oh yeah?" I kept my voice as light as possible.

"Yeah. He asked me if *you* had told me anything about a certain case that he's currently investigating. For some reason, he thought maybe you would have told me that you are a suspect in a missing person's investigation."

Pulling into an empty parking lot, I parked the truck. This was a conversation that needed my full attention. I turned to look at Adriane.

"I'm sorry I didn't tell you," I started, but before I could continue, Adriane threw her hands up.

"I wanted you to say that it wasn't true! I needed you to tell me you have nothing to do with that girl's disappearance!" She dropped her head into her hands.

"I didn't think I *needed* to say that! I'm not, though! They haven't even found Ally's body yet, so there's a chance..."

I trailed off. There was no chance that she was still alive, but I couldn't let that small sliver of hope go. Not yet.

Adriane lifted her head but wouldn't look me in the eye. "And, what, you thought you could use me to find out how much the cops knew about the case? How am I not supposed to think you're hiding something?"

"That's not why I chose to hang out with you. But I've been trying so hard to remember what happened the night Ally died, I couldn't *not* ask if the police had any more information than I did. It's been driving me crazy." I kept my gaze pinned on my hands in my lap, too afraid to see the look on Adriane's face.

"You can't even remember whether or not you killed her," she whispered, as if saying it too loud would startle me or something. It wasn't anything I hadn't already thought of myself. "I want to believe you when you say you didn't, but I think I need some time to think about all this before I decide whether I can trust you or not. You haven't exactly been honest with me since we met."

"Please, don't end this," I pleaded.

Adriane shook her head. "I'm sorry, Zac. I can't do this. Can you please take me home?"

I didn't bother arguing. I drove back out onto the road and drove to Adriane's house. She didn't even say goodbye when she got out of my truck, and I couldn't blame her.

The whole ride home I kept thinking the grief would hit me, but instead I felt cold, empty, and more alone than ever. I had nothing to cry over because I had nothing left to lose.

Mom had saved me a plate and it was still warm when I sat at the counter to eat it.

"Hey, sweetie. What happened?" She came up behind me and put her hand on my shoulder.

"I'll talk about it in therapy tomorrow," I snapped.

Mom's grip on my shoulder tightened before she let go and I heard her footsteps going up the stairs.

I knew it wasn't her fault that I'd kept too many secrets from Adriane, and I shouldn't have taken it out on her, but I didn't apologize. I ate my food in silence and then went to bed.

When I checked my texts in the morning, I half expected one from Adriane, but the only text I had was from Josh, reminding me of a party at Aaron's that weekend. I would go, if only to take my mind off everything.

Chapter Twelve
Alana
Six days before

Before school, I wandered the halls looking for Jake in hopes of fixing things. Coming around a corner, I ran first into Connor instead.

"Ohmigosh. I am so sorry." I helped pick up his books that had fallen to the floor. "I'm a little out of sorts today."

"It's fine. I heard about you and Jake, I'm sorry." He stuffed all his books into his backpack.

"Oh, he told you." I wasn't sure why that bothered me so much.

"Yeah, we hung out yesterday and he mentioned it. He seemed really upset about it."

"Hmm. Have you seen him today?"

"No, sorry." Connor shook his head.

The bell rang and we parted ways.

At the end of the day, I noticed Jake's truck in the parking lot, and decided I would wait for him there. He had to show up eventually if he wanted to go home. I only had to wait about five minutes before he came out to his truck. When he saw me, he looked sheepish and hesitant to approach me, but he did.

"Hey, Jake." I broke the awkward silence. "I wanted to talk to you." Jake nodded and opened the passenger door of his truck for me to get in. He hopped into the driver's seat, and finally spoke.

"I love you, Ally, and I don't want to lose you." His voice wavered. "I am so sorry about everything I said the other night, I wish I could take it back, but I can't."

"I know. It's okay. I've had a little bit of time to think about it, and I think I was too harsh yesterday. I should have accepted your apology. However, I'm still not sure I want to get back into a relationship with you yet. It still hurts to think about having to listen to you yelling at me." I pinched the bridge of my nose, hoping to hold back the tears.

"Ally, I hate seeing you like this." Jake pulled me closer to him.

"It's hard, because you're usually the reason that I get like this," I said.

Jake let go of me so that he could look into my eyes.

"I could never hurt you again like this, Ally. You must know that." Jake's eyes were pleading.

"I don't... I don't think I can be with you again yet. I can give you another chance. Just know that you will be on thin ice with me, and we are not back together yet." I was not going to let him walk all over me anymore. Jake grinned from ear to ear.

"Oh, Ally, thank you! I love you! I promise I won't do anything to hurt you ever again!" Jake kissed me and started his truck.

We hung out in my room for the rest of the day. At first, we sat on the edge of my bed together. I was hesitant to get too close to him, afraid I would let down my barrier and forget that he was supposed to be winning me back.

"So... does thin ice mean I can't kiss you?" Jake asked, smiling. I pretended to think about it for a second, and then kissed him.

He grinned and said, "I knew you wouldn't be able to resist."

"Oh, shut up." I laughed and rolled my eyes.

Jake readjusted so he was lying on the bed, propped up by the pillows. I stayed on the edge of the bed, but I leaned back, resting my head on his chest.

After a minute or so, I burst out laughing and said, "This is actually quite uncomfortable." I moved so that I was lying next to him and leaned my head on his shoulder. Jake reached for my hand, and I let him hold it.

We talked about random things for a little while, and then fell asleep. One second, I was propped up in bed with the sun streaming through the window, and the next I was in a pitch-black room with Jake's arms around me and our legs tangled together.

I laid there, content, for a few minutes, until my phone vibrated, sounding like thunder in the silent room. The light that shone from it was like staring into the sun after coming out of a cave. I grabbed it off the bedside table and shoved it under my pillow. Jake stirred.

"Jake?" I whispered into the silence.

"Yeah?" he responded.

"I'm going to turn on the light." I reached toward where I knew my lamp was and flipped the switch.

"Ugh." Jake buried his face into the pillows. "It's so bright."

The message on my phone was from Dianna, and it said *Dinner's ready.* Jake's head was on my shoulder, and he read the message.

"You want to stay for dinner?" I asked, hoping he would say yes.

"Sure." Jake kissed my cheek, and we reluctantly got out of bed.

When we were seated at the table, I realized how strange it was that we were all eating dinner together. Dianna, Clyde, Jake, and myself.

"What have you two kiddies been up to cooped up in that room all day?" Clyde asked. His smirk made me cringe.

"Sleeping," Jake answered.

"Yeah, sure," Clyde laughed, and Dianna looked as uncomfortable as I felt.

"Believe what you want, but we were really sleeping." I reached for a cheeseburger and put it on my plate.

"How was school today, Ally?" Dianna asked.

I cocked an eyebrow; *why is she pretending to care?*

I shrugged, not offering anything else.

"Okay. Well, I am glad you can't even give me any information on what you're doing in that damn school after everything I do for you," Dianna grumbled.

"Just tell her what you did today, Alana!" Clyde rubbed Dianna's back to comfort her.

"I went to classes, I did stupid work, and I talked to some people. It was like any other day at school." I tried to stay as calm as possible.

"Thank you," Dianna said, and I rolled my eyes. It seemed this was what we went through any time we were all together.

"How was your day, honey?" Clyde asked Dianna, who shrugged.

So, she can get away with that, but I can't? Hypocrite, I thought.

After dinner, Jake had to leave. I tried to convince him to stay, putting on my best sad puppy face, but his parents wanted him home, so I had to let him go.

The next few days went by quickly. I only had a four-day week. Thursday, I spent the whole day looking at the clock because I couldn't wait to be home. Both Mariah and Jake were not at school that day, and I wasn't risking mucking things up with Jake by asking Connor for a ride, knowing he would tell Jake since they were best friends. So, I decided to ask Zac for a ride home. We were trying to patch things up anyway, and there was less of a chance Jake would find out.

"Hey Zac." I approached him as he left the school.

"Oh, hey, Ally." He smiled brightly. "What's up?"

"Do you mind bringing me home today?" I asked.

"I didn't drive today, I walked. But you can walk with me if you want," he said, hopefully.

I nodded and we started walking. Once we reached their road, we automatically veered off toward the park. It was our go-to spot back when we were best friends.

"I've missed coming here and hanging out," I said, and Zac nodded. "I'm really sorry about the other day, you know, shoving you and all." I smiled sheepishly, making Zac laugh.

"Oh, don't worry about that. I probably deserved it." The rest of the conversation went much more smoothly. It was as if no time had passed at all since we stopped being friends.

I loved that I could be completely myself with Zac. It was hard for me to be that way with Jake anymore. I was always afraid if I made one wrong move, he would leave. There was no reason for me to worry about that anymore. I knew that I had Mariah and Zac there if anything happened with Jake. Everything felt right at that moment.

Zac walked me back to my house. When I stepped inside, I noticed something was off. I peeked into the kitchen and realized what it was. My dad sat at the bar with Clyde.

I stood rooted to my spot staring at them sitting there, silently. Clyde was rigid and I could tell he was pissed. Dianna wasn't home yet, and I imagined them sitting there for two more hours until she arrived. Creeping back out of the front door, I ran down the steps.

Halfway down the street, I realized it was freezing outside. I'd dropped my jacket on the floor in the house, but I wasn't going back there. The house where I could still see my dad cooking in the kitchen, sleeping on the couch, or racing me up the stairs to see who would reach the top first. He had always let me win, but I knew that none of that really meant anything to him. A tear trickled down my cheek, and I wiped it away. He didn't deserve to be with Dianna.

Who does he think he is, coming back into our lives so abruptly, thinking we will let him back in? I thought.

My phone vibrated in my pocket, and I sighed in relief when I saw Jake's name on the screen.

"Hey, can you come pick me up?" I needed to get as far away from that house as possible.

"Yeah. I just left Connor's. I'll be there in a minute."

"I'm not at my house; I'm at the end of my street," I said; glad I wouldn't have to wait out in the cold for too much longer.

"All right, I'm almost there." His truck was coming toward me, so I hung up. His truck rumbled to a stop beside me and I hopped into the passenger seat. Knowing that Dianna and my dad would be trying to call me, I silenced my phone and tossed it onto the floor. I didn't need it now that I was with Jake.

Jake leaned over and kissed me. "What's up?" he asked as he turned his gaze back to the road.

"Nothing. I needed to get away from home." I continued looking out the window as we drove toward Jake's house.

"Perfect. My parents are on vacation somewhere in South America or something, so I'm having a party tonight," Jake said. It was funny how he always planned these things at the last minute, or maybe he always told me last. "Dad said he couldn't stand to be near me for another minute, and they left again," Jake shrugged. "Works for me. I couldn't care less when and where they go."

I peeked over at him and could see the hurt in his eyes but knew that he would never admit it.

"Well, a party sounds like just what we need. A good way to keep our minds off our parents." I put my hand on his. He smiled and lifted my hand to his lips.

"I love you, Ally," he murmured.

My heart fluttered in my chest.

"You are doing an awfully good job of winning me back." I couldn't help but smile. It felt like the perfect moment. I closed my eyes and leaned my head on Jake's shoulder. Jake's phone rang in his cup holder, and I grabbed it.

"I got it," I said, and saw the name that flashed across the screen: *Katrina.* Jake snatched it out of my hand.

"No, I got it." Jake answered his phone. "Hello... I can't talk right now... Yeah... See you tonight." He hung up.

"Who was that?" I pretended I didn't already know.

"Connor," Jake lied.

"What did he want?" I asked casually.

"None of your goddamn business," Jake snapped.

I moved away from him. Of course, he had to ruin yet another moment.

"I'm sorry," I muttered.

"What was that?" Jake snarled.

I whipped around to face him again. "I said I am *sorry.* I'm sorry that I care about what goes on in my boyfriend's life. Even though he lies to me and doesn't care if he hurts me. I thought you said that if I gave you another chance, you would never hurt me again?" Tears ran down my face, and I turned back to the window. I hated to let him see me cry.

"I can take you home if that's what you want," Jake said, obviously not caring that he had hurt me, yet again.

"No, that's not what I want," I said. I was silent for the rest of the ride to Jake's house. When we got there, some of Jake's friends were rolling in the kegs. I saw Connor among them, and I waved solemnly. Waving back, he continued to lift one of the kegs off his truck bed with Joe. They had a tarp in the back of his truck that they used to cover all the kegs when they brought them over. I couldn't imagine that people didn't still know exactly what was under those tarps when they drove by.

"I'm going to go help the guys. You can go inside or whatever," Jake told me. I nodded, getting out of Jake's truck, and nearly fell on my face.

"Crap," I murmured. I'd torn my jeans and cut open my knee on a rock. Sitting on the ground, I grabbed a tissue from a compartment in Jake's truck door and dabbed my knee. It wasn't too bad, there was minimal blood.

"Hey, you okay?" Connor crouched down beside me, looking at my knee.

"Yeah, I'm fine. Just a scratch." I tried to force a smile.

"Good." Connor stood back up and extended his hand out to me. I gratefully took it, and he pulled me to my feet.

"Today is not my day." I laughed nervously. Jake was watching, and he would not like me talking to Connor, but Jake and I were not technically together, and he'd thoroughly pissed me off.

"Sorry to hear that. How are you doing?" Connor asked with real concern in his voice.

"Stupid." I rolled my eyes.

"Excuse me?" Connor's brows pinched together in confusion, making me laugh again.

"No, sorry. I feel stupid," I explained, thinking about how I had let Jake back into my life so easily.

"Oh, I see," Connor laughed. "That can happen. I've been plenty stupid over the years," he teased.

"Eh hem." Jake cleared his throat. "Alana, shouldn't you be going inside?" Jake's voice was strained, and I could sense that he was holding back his anger.

"Fine." I threw my hands up and stormed inside.

When it started getting dark and the lights came on, people began arriving. The music was blaring, and the alcohol was pouring. Connor and I stayed as far away from each other as possible. Connor joined his friends, and I went straight to the kitchen. One of Jake's friends handed me a cup and filled it from the keg.

"Do you know where Jake is?" I asked him.

"You might need a couple more refills before you go see him," he said. I faked a laugh, then chugged my beer.

"Fill her up then!" I grinned, walking away once my cup was full again.

In the living room, people were taking shots. I sat on the couch and waited for the shot glass in front of me to be filled. Everyone else drank theirs right away. I finished off the beer in my hand first and took my shot. It tasted terrible. I was beginning to feel drunk, but my stomach was in a terrible state from chugging those beers.

I stood from the couch and stumbled away. As I crossed into the next room, I tripped over someone's shoe that was in the middle of the hallway and fell to the floor, deciding to lay there for a while. *Maybe no one will notice if I lay here forever. Maybe I'll disappear.* I closed my eyes and listened to the music swirling around me.

Realizing I was laying in some kind of puddle of spilled alcohol, I sat up and scrunched my nose. A couple of people were staring at me like I was crazy.

I guess I should change. I went up to the guest room where I had extra clothes but wound up in Jake's room. The door had been closed, but I pushed it open and walked over to the dresser. Once I was there, I realized my mistake and that there was someone else in the room. Nearly knocking down the whole dresser, I jumped at the sight of Jake at the window.

"Ohmigosh," my words all ran together. I clutched my chest. "You scared the crap out of me."

"Sorry," he muttered. I backed out of the room and grabbed a new set of clothes from the dresser in the guest room, then went back to Jake's room.

"I may have drunk those beers a bit too fast." I laughed as I stumbled over to Jake. It didn't take much alcohol for me to start losing my balance and footing. I was already clumsy enough as it was.

"Yeah, I think so. Your shirt is on backwards," Jake pointed out, making me laugh.

"That could happen to anyone! It was dark in the room." Jake took my dirty clothes and put them into the laundry basket.

"I'll take care of those in the morning," he said.

"Thanks." I tried to stop myself from swaying. My stomach grumbled. I hadn't had anything to eat since lunch. A wave of nausea came over me and my hand flew up to my mouth. Running to the bathroom, I barely made it in time before I got sick. Jake stood in the doorway.

"I guess you'll be staying the night," he said matter-of-factly. I didn't bother to answer as I hovered over the toilet. Jake knelt beside me and grabbed one of my hair-ties off his sink. He pulled back my hair for me.

Tears welled in my eyes as the pain of everything that had happened that day hit. My dad was waiting for me at home. My boyfriend was a jerk, but he was also the sweetest boy I'd ever met when he wanted to be. Connor was avoiding me, and now I was so sick I couldn't move because I'd drunk too fast. My stomach ached as a reminder of that last point.

"We'll talk later, when you're feeling better." Jake rubbed my back. "I'm going to go get you some water." He stood and left.

I didn't want to wait around for Jake to come back. It wasn't like I was *actually* drunk; I needed some food and water, and I'd be back in tip-top shape. So, I headed for the kitchen to find myself a snack.

Once I finished off a whole sleeve of crackers and a glass of water, I felt ten times better. But that didn't mean I was ready for another drink. The beer had really ruined me for the night.

Looking out the window, my gaze stopped at the pool, where a few people were hanging out in the lounge chairs.

"I wanna go swimming," I said to no one. I pushed myself off the floor where I'd been hiding out while I snacked and headed outside.

There were a lot of people in the pool already. Connor was making out with a girl in one of the lounge chairs and I wasn't sure why it affected me so much, but jealousy reared its head. I walked over to the edge of the pool and as I decided *not* to go in, I lost my balance and fell forward.

Now I'm going to have to change again was my first thought. *Or maybe, I can stay in the water...* Making no effort to swim to the surface, I sank to the bottom.

The water was having a very sobering effect on me. I opened my eyes and saw all the people around me, oblivious to me sitting at the bottom of the pool. Someone lifted me from behind and I struggled to get free. Once I was at the surface, I spluttered and turned to my unwanted savior.

Connor's hair dripped water down his face as he stared back at me.

"What are you doing?" he spluttered, his arms still around me, as if he worried I might try to go back down to the bottom of the pool.

I bit my lip and pulled away from him. "I'm fine," I said. My teeth chattered as a cold wind whipped around us. My head felt much clearer now, and my stomach had calmed down.

Connor's gaze softened and he reached out to me.

"Let me help you-"

"I don't want your help." I swam away from him toward the edge of the pool.

"Alana!" Jake's voice boomed over the surface of the water as he walked out the kitchen door.

Slowly, I submerged back into the water.

I don't want to deal with this, I thought.

When I came back up, Jake was waiting on the edge of the pool.

"Get out of the water." He had his arms crossed and looked so serious; I couldn't help but laugh.

"You get *in*!" I took a step closer to him and saw the hint of a smile on his face. "Please?" I pouted.

He rolled his eyes, but took his shirt off and jumped in. I swam over to him and put my arms around his neck.

"I only got in to take you out." Jake put his arms around my waist and pulled me toward the steps that led out of the pool, where Connor was currently drying the lounge chair with that girl.

"No!" I pulled away from him, giggling. "I want to swim! We never swim!" Wriggling free from his embrace, she swam to the edge of the pool. The adrenaline of trying to make Connor as jealous as I'd been had me feeling more buzzed than the alcohol.

"Come and get me," I teased Jake, but I was still looking at Connor. When Jake reached me, I pushed him against the side of the pool and kissed him. I looked back at Connor, and he was watching me. Then I let Jake lead me out of the pool.

"Let's get you dried off." Jake grabbed a towel off a chair and put it around my shoulders.

"Can we go up to your room now? I want to change." I held the towel tightly, feeling the cold deep in my bones. Jake nodded and kissed my forehead. It felt forced and for once, I wished he wasn't the one standing with me. Jake took my hand

and led me to his room. I went to the window first to look for Connor, but he wasn't by the pool anymore.

"I want to go to bed," I said quietly. Jake hugged me from behind and I turned to him. "I'm so sorry," I mumbled into his shoulder.

"Don't worry about it." Jake hugged me tighter and then let me go. "You should change and get to sleep. I'll be downstairs if you need me."

I watched him go and then crumpled on the floor. Why did I want Connor so badly when Jake was finally being nice to me? It didn't make any sense.

I pulled off my pants and curled up under my towel. Maybe I had a fairy godmother that would magically bring more clothes to me and solve all my problems. *Unlikely.* I went over to the guest room, but instead of grabbing more clothes, I curled up in my towel on the bed.

There was a hesitant knock on the door. I stood to answer it, realizing I was only wearing my bra and underwear. I grabbed the towel and wrapped it around myself again.

"Come in," I hollered over the music that thrummed through the whole house. The door opened and Connor stepped into the room, shutting the door behind him. My face flushed and I held the towel more tightly around myself. Everything I had done up to that point felt so embarrassing.

"Jake said it would be all right if I came to check on you," Connor said, rubbing the back of his neck.

"That's weird. I thought he would never let you near me again." I dipped my head, letting my hair partially hide my face. I couldn't bear to let Connor see my true feelings.

"Yeah. I thought so too." It was silent for a minute, and then he spoke again. "I wanted to make sure you were okay after... Everything."

"I'm surprised your friend let you leave her side long enough to come up here." My voice wavered as I fought back tears.

"I'm sorry I was with another girl, but I don't really see what that has to do with you." Connor started to leave.

"No! Please stay. I'm sorry. You're right. It's not like we're dating or anything."

He stopped and turned back to me, but I looked away again, hiding my feelings. He sat on the bed beside me, gazing up at me.

"Are you okay?" He took my hand in his.

"Yes. No. Maybe, I don't know," I sighed. I was feeling almost back to myself again, but even the tiniest bit of alcohol meant I had no real control over what came out of my mouth. I did my best to keep my mouth shut when something I wanted to say bubbled to the surface.

"Maybe we should talk tomorrow." Connor grinned and I couldn't help but smile back. "Goodnight, Ally." Connor stood up and I watched him walk toward the door.

"Wait." He stopped.

I walked over to him, took his face in my hands, and kissed him. He put his arms around me, and I realized that I'd let go of my towel, but I didn't care about that anymore. Connor lifted me onto the bed and continued to kiss me.

Chapter Thirteen
Zac

"Is there anything else you want to talk about?" my therapist asked.

I'd already told her about my falling out with Adriane, which she had wanted to talk about much longer than I ever would.

"Nope." I would admit, there was probably a lot I *should* talk about, but I wasn't in the mood for that. I needed to get out of that office. It was too warm there, and the chair I sat in was too soft. I sank way further down in it than I'd like. It was almost like it was trying to suck me in and keep me there until I agreed to spill all my secrets.

"Well, I guess I'll see you next week then." She smiled brightly.

"Next week?" I hadn't made any follow up appointments that I knew of.

"Yes. Your mother scheduled them out a few weeks for you." She stood and headed for the door, opening it for me.

Of course. Mom wouldn't trust me to make my own appointments after I'd failed to do that the last time.

"See you next week," I muttered as I left the office.

In my truck, I studied my map of different wooded areas in town again. One of the largest areas was around Aaron's house. The party on Saturday would give me the perfect opportunity to do a little searching while everyone else was distracted. I didn't want to have to explain myself to anyone. I tucked my map away and drove home.

The next few days dragged on as I waited for the opportunity to look for Ally again. Adriane avoided me in the halls, and I didn't go looking for her. If she needed time to think, I'd give it to her.

On Saturday night, my friends showed up around eight to pick me up for the party.

"So, Michael has offered to be our designated driver for the night," Josh said.

Jess and Katrina both cackled in the back seat of the van. Michael wasn't exactly the most reliable of our group.

"I'm not so sure I trust my life in his hands," I joked.

"Hey, I'm a great driver!" Michael defended himself.

"Yeah, as long as you don't drink anything, which seems to always be a problem for you," Josh added, and then said, "but don't worry because I can't drink tonight anyway. I have this family thing tomorrow morning that I have to be awake for. I'll be the driver tonight. Michael can drive next time."

"Works for me." Michael shrugged.

There was already a good number of people at Aaron's house when we arrived.

Music blared in the living room. I could see the ripples in the drinks from the vibrations of the bass. The music came from Connor and Joe playing Rock Band. They'd turned the television up as loud as it could go. I was surprised to see them there, but Katrina and Joe *were* dating. Katrina joined them as the singer, much to my dismay.

"We're about to want to vacate the area," Jess teased as she watched her sister join the game. "Unless you want to punish your ears."

Mariah stood across the room with a group of girls I recognized from school. She waved and I waved back before heading to the bar to greet Aaron. He was mixing drinks for a couple of people.

I sat on one of the tall, black bar stools, scanning the room to see if Adriane was there. She was nowhere in sight, although Josh was talking with Jake near the kitchen. I almost had to do a double take. Jake must have tagged along with Connor. Apparently, our friend groups had merged while I'd been distracted by trying to find Ally. I turned back to Aaron.

"Want a drink?" Aaron asked without looking up from the bar.

"Yes, please." I'd need some liquid courage to sneak out of the party and go hunting for Ally's body. For some reason, doing it at night scared me a whole lot more than when I'd searched during the day. It wasn't like it changed the results of my search at all.

I chugged my drink, and Aaron had refilled it before I could ask for more. I was about to sneak away and start my search, but Josh crossed my path and intercepted me.

"Play pong with me," he said. He gripped my upper arm as if this was something more serious than a game of beer pong.

I nodded. "All right, man." I followed him over to the table and stood on the opposite side to him. Connor joined me on my side, and Joe was with Josh. I don't think I had ever talked to Connor before.

For the first few rounds, we continued not to talk. Until we'd each finished a couple shots Aaron had delivered to us, and then neither of us could *stop* talking. I hadn't planned on getting too drunk, since I still wanted to go out looking for Ally, but I also didn't want to raise any red flags. Me refusing a shot would have been a definite red flag. Maybe. Or maybe I wanted to put off my search for as long as possible.

"I think I get better at this the drunker I get," Connor said, laughing. "Watch." He sunk his next ball in the center cup.

I burst out laughing. Josh didn't find it quite as funny as he chugged his beer.

"I'm glad you finally decided to grace us with your presence. I needed a good pong partner," I joked.

"I don't usually drink all that much," Connor said, and the smile slipped from his face. "With Ally gone..." He trailed off. "Sorry, I know you two were friends."

I hiccupped and put my hand to my mouth before saying, "I didn't realize you were close with her."

"We had just started seeing each other casually, she didn't want to rush into anything right after Jake."

Josh shook the table enough to get our attention.

"Your turn," he said.

A thought struck me as I stared across the table at Josh.

"You're supposed to be the DD! Why the hell are you drinking?" I yelled over the music.

"Don' worry 'bout it." Josh waved his hand.

Shaking my head, I said, "Well let's hope Aaron has a few extra beds tonight." I stepped away from the table. "I'm calling it. I need another drink," I lied. It was time I started my search of the woods outside. If I didn't do it right then, I never would.

The game seemed to dissolve after I left.

I headed for the kitchen, which had a back door to the patio. I could slip away easily from there and into the woods.

Katrina waved to me as I made my way through the living room. When I passed her by, I noticed her eyes glazing over, and she was swaying.

"Hey, Katrina. Have you seen Jess?" He noticed her eyes were glazed, so she would not be the one to ask to drive them home.

"Ugh, I hate the smell of the beer I puked up," she complained, and I muffled my laugh as I kept walking.

I had almost made it to the back door when I ran into Mariah.

"Oh, Zac." She seemed flustered. "Have you seen Josh?" Her hand flew up to her mouth and she shook her head.

"What's wrong?" I asked.

"Nothing. We got in a fight earlier and I... You know what, never mind. It's really nothing." She walked away before I could ask any more questions. But the fact that they had got into a fight explained why he was drinking when he said he wouldn't.

I was finally at the backdoor and no one was around, so I cracked it and slipped outside. The cool air hit me like a wave and sobered me up slightly. Thankfully the wind wasn't too bad that night, but it was still cold, and my flannel only did so much to hold in my warmth.

Jogging away from the house, I reached the first line of trees and pulled out my phone. The flashlight was a necessity since it was pitch black beneath the moonless sky.

"What are you doing?"

I jumped and whipped around as Connor came up behind me.

"Give a guy a warning next time," I gasped, still trying to catch my breath as I held my hand to my chest. My heart was beating so fast I thought it might burst.

"I thought I did," he said, lifting a shoulder. "So, what are you doing?"

I considered lying, but I saw no point in it. Connor had told me he and Ally were dating, so I knew he cared about her. Maybe it would be nice to have someone with me while I searched for her in case I found her. I didn't know what I would do if that actually happened.

"I'm looking for Ally," I admitted. "I've *been* looking for her ever since she disappeared. Well, her body, I guess." I cringed as I said it. I hated to talk about her as if she was dead, even if it was true.

A puff of Connor's breath was visible in the cold.

"Oh." His gaze flicked to the trees. "Do you really think someone would have buried her here?"

"Honestly? Yeah. This is one of the largest wooded areas in town, and no one ever comes out here because Aaron's family owns most of the property. So, perfect place to hide something, or someone, you never want to be found."

"Seems like you've thought this through," he said.

"Thankfully I made my plan pre-drinking, otherwise I don't think I'd be able to do that much idea forming right now."

"Lead the way," Connor said.

"You sure you want to come with me?" I couldn't imagine this was how he wanted to spend his Saturday night; chasing ghosts with some guy he'd never spent more than five seconds with before that night.

"Absolutely not. But I'm doing it anyway. Blame the alcohol, or the grief. Can't be sure which is in control right now."

Without waiting to see if he'd change his mind, I started a path through the woods. I'd decided before I arrived at Aaron's that the most likely place someone would bury a body would be to the left of his house, since it was more accessible from the road. Someone wouldn't necessarily have to go down the driveway and alert whoever was home that they were there.

Connor and I split up and searched for at least an hour before we came back together with nothing to show for it.

"Let's do one last pass closer to the middle," I suggested.

Connor sighed. "All right, but then I have to go inside. My fingers are freezing." He flexed his hand that wasn't holding his phone for a flashlight.

"A few more minutes," I said, leading the way toward a new area we hadn't walked through yet.

We were at least a ten-minute walk from the house and closer to the main road, so occasionally, headlights shone through the trees.

I moved further from the road where the headlights wouldn't reach. "We can start looking here." I didn't look back and kept walking, but there was a small crash and Connor cursed.

"Damn roots."

I turned back to help him up. His phone must have dropped, because I couldn't see his flashlight anymore, and I had to pass my flashlight over the area a few times before I spotted him.

"I don't think it was really a root, it was too soft, but I can't look," Connor said, his voice tight and he still laid on the ground with his eyes tightly shut. "I think I'm going to throw up. Tell me what it was."

I moved closer. There was a low mound of dirt about the same size as Connor that he laid across. Looking near his boots, I noticed a color that didn't belong.

"I don't think-"

"No don't tell me," Connor gasped. "Help me up first."

I reached down and grasped his hand, helping him to his feet. He turned away from where he'd fallen and bent down, resting his hands on his knees.

I crouched down beside the slice of pink I saw in the dirt. Carefully brushing some of the dirt away, I realized it was fabric.

"Yay! I knew you'd come down from the tower eventually." Ally hugged me. Her pink jacket's zipper caught on my sleeve.

"Yay," I said sarcastically as I unhooked her zipper, and she stepped back. "I'm not friends with any of these people, Ally."

"Well, you should try to become friends with some of them. You're friends with Mariah." Ally pulled Mariah over to her.

"I was talking to someone, Ally." Mariah laughed.

"Sorry, but aren't you and Zac friends?" Ally asked.

"Yeah, why?" Mariah glanced at me.

"He says he's not friends with anyone here," Ally told her. Mariah laughed and rolled her eyes, then she turned back to Jess, and they both walked off.

"I think I'm going to go home. It's almost nine anyway." I started walking away.

"No! Please stay!" she pleaded.

"Fine. Where's Jake?" I knew he was the reason we were there.

"He went for a walk with a couple other people. Hey look! It's..." She was cut off by someone screaming.

"Zac?" Connor was still bent over beside me, but he'd turned his head to look at me. "What is it?"

"It's her jacket." My voice was barely more than a whisper. "I'm pretty sure." Breathing had become much harder than I'd ever remembered it being, and I couldn't move any of my limbs, as if they'd been locked in place.

Connor cursed and turned around, heaving. Thankfully it seemed like nothing was coming up.

I stared down at the pink fabric, tempted to pull it free from the dirt, but I feared what might come up with it. From the size of the mound of dirt, there was only one thing that could be buried beneath it.

After a while my knees screamed from crouching there, avoiding the inevitable. Once we called the police and they came out here, it would be over. Ally would be officially declared dead, and there would be no chance of her coming back. I hadn't realized how strong the hope in me was that I'd find her alive somehow, until it had been snuffed out.

Tears burned my eyes as I tried to keep them from falling.

"Maybe it's not hers," Connor said. "Maybe we're wrong."

I wanted to believe his words. I wanted them to be true. This wasn't Ally's jacket, but a random scrap of pink fabric. But I knew deep down, I was right.

"It's hers," I insisted.

"What do we do?" Connor still refused to look at the mound of dirt, even though it hid the horror beneath.

What if the killer is at the party? The party.

"I'm texting Aaron to let him know what happened so he can clear everyone out before the police come." I wrote out the text, making sure to tell Aaron not to let anyone know the real reason the party was ending. I didn't want to tip off the killer if they were at the party.

Aaron texted back almost immediately. *Shit. I'll get everyone out. Do what you gotta do,* he wrote.

Connor sat on the ground, back to Ally, his knees pulled up to his chest.

"I'll give it ten minutes and call," I said. "What's ten minutes when she's been here for weeks already." A forceful laugh came from me, though I'd no idea what there was to laugh at. I sat beside Connor, and we waited out the minutes in silence.

My heart beat so loudly in my chest, I was surprised Connor didn't mention it, but then again, maybe his own heartbeat was drowning the sound of mine out.

"I think I wouldn't be nearly as calm if I hadn't been drinking," Connor said after I called the police. "I don't think it's sunk in yet."

"Well, we should wait until they dig this up and confirm our suspicions before we jump to any conclusions." I was still in denial and probably would be even after they dug up Ally's body.

~

The next day I woke up to my phone vibrating under my pillow. Mom came and picked me up after the police arrived and they made Connor and I leave the scene. They'd thoroughly questioned us first, asking why we were in the woods to begin with, and we'd told them the truth. Mostly. We avoided any mention of the party and said we were hanging out at Aaron's when we had the idea of searching the woods for Ally.

I groaned and reached under my pillow, retrieving my phone. There was a text from Connor.

It's her. They confirmed it.

And he'd sent along the news article announcing it too.

I draped my arm over my eyes, wishing I could go back to sleep and wake up again in an alternate universe. One where Ally had made it back to my house that night, and I never thought about whether I might be capable of murdering my best friend.

Wait. No. I didn't kill her.

I shook my head and got out of bed, going to the shower in hopes that I could wash away the memory of finding Ally.

Chapter Fourteen
Alana
Two days before

"Alana," Jake called through the door.

Connor and I both shot out of bed.

"Uh, hold on a sec. I'm, um, changing," I called back, my voice cracking.

Jake waited a few more seconds but opened the door to find Connor pulling on his pants and me throwing on a shirt.

"Oh, hi," I squeaked as Jake stood in the doorway with his jaw dropped.

"Just because we broke up, doesn't mean you had my permission to screw my best friend," he spoke calmly, which was more troubling than if he yelled at me.

I bit my lip. "I know, I..."

"You're a slut," he interrupted me. "I am so glad we broke up."

"Woah, man. Calm down." Connor stepped forward.

Jake whirled on him. "Don't tell me to calm down. I thought you were my best friend, I guess I was wrong. My best friend wouldn't sleep with my ex-girlfriend." Jake took a step toward Connor and punched him square in the jaw.

"Jake! Leave him alone! I did this. I kissed him first!" I put myself between them.

"I don't believe you! Connor has always wanted you, ever since we started dating. I should have never let him near you." Jake fumed.

"I swear! I wouldn't lie to you." I paused, not sure what to say next.

"Don't even start with that! I've never had your whole heart, there has always been someone else! I lived with that because I thought someday you would get over it." Jake balled his hands into fists at his sides.

"Huh?" I had no idea what he was talking about.

He rolled his eyes. "Don't tell me you don't remember when you loved Zac? That was when we first started dating. I saw the way you looked at him. There was a short time when I thought you were finally over him, and Connor came along. I didn't think you would ever betray me. I was wrong."

"I'm sorry, you're right," I responded, deflated.

Apparently, that was not what he had wanted to hear, and he stormed out of the room.

"Is what he said true?" I asked Connor.

"Well, you agreed with him, so, yes?" he answered, unsure.

"No, I mean what he said about you. That you've 'wanted' me since Jake and I started dating."

"I wouldn't say that I *wanted* you."

I scoffed and left the room. Jake paused his pacing to glare at me, but I couldn't even look him in the eye.

"I have to go." I ran down the stairs.

I glanced at the clock. It was four in the morning, and people were passed out on the couches, and a few on tables.

Outside, I sat on the edge of the pool. It was the last place I had been before I'd messed everything up. If only Connor hadn't been there to help me out of the pool, I could have stayed on the bottom and never come up. That would have made everyone's lives easier.

I dipped my feet into the water, and it sent a chill up through my body. Before I considered what I was doing, I slipped into the water. The shock stole my breath and made everything seem crystal clear. If I stayed at the bottom of the pool, I would never have to face my dad. Slowly, I sank beneath the surface and let my thoughts slip away.

A sense of calmness made me feel lighter than I ever had. But then, different thoughts came creeping in. Who would Mariah talk to when she needed advice? Who would take care of Dianna when Clyde didn't come home from 'work' at night? And I'd just become friends with Zac again. And Connor...

I pushed myself back to the surface and gasped for air. There were more important people to worry about than my dad, or Jake, or even myself. I climbed out of the pool and grabbed the towel that someone had left on one of the chairs. Wrapping the towel around myself, I went back inside, hurrying upstairs where I found Jake in the guest room staring out the window.

"I saw you in the pool. What were you doing? Trying to drown yourself?" Jake continued to stare out the window.

"What if I was? You weren't going to try to save me?" I asked, almost laughing at the thought of that.

"Oh, I sent Connor down there to help you," Jake said scornfully. "Apparently, he didn't care enough to save you because I didn't see him go outside. I wonder where he got to."

"You have no right to be angry with me!" I yelled, unable to contain my frustration with him any longer. He gave me a look of disgust, but I pushed on. "How could you be so angry with me, when you cheated on me first?!"

"We were trying to work things out and then you go and sleep with Connor. Connor is my best friend!" Jake yelled back.

"So what! I technically broke up with you days ago! You didn't even *wait* until we broke up to cheat on me!" I reminded him.

"Have you not been listening to anything I have said tonight? I knew you didn't love me, not really, anyway. It was over between us the moment you started talking to Zac again."

"So, I guess that's it. We're not together and you are free to be with Katrina." I narrowed my eyes at him.

"And you to be with Connor, or Zac, or both. What do I care?" Jake rebuked.

"Can I at least put some clothes on?" I asked. Jake groaned but left me alone in the room so I could get dressed.

When I left the room, I went in search of Connor. Jake had sent him to the pool, but he hadn't shown up. I found him sitting in his truck and climbed into the passenger seat, sliding into the middle to be near him.

"Jake said he sent you down to the pool. Why didn't you come?" I asked, not like I *needed* him, or anything.

"I saw you come back up." Connor's face was solemn.

"Oh. Well, why didn't you stay?" I twisted my hands in my lap.

"You would rather drown yourself than be with me, that's why I didn't stay. You didn't even let me finish earlier, when you asked if I've always wanted to be with you." Connor's hands were trembling on the wheel.

"You said you didn't," I reminded him.

"Yeah, I said I wouldn't say that I *wanted* you. I did, I wanted you. But I hardly knew you. I wanted to get to know you, and now that I have, I *do* want you, but you don't want me." Connor rested his head on the wheel.

I put my hand on his arm. "I wasn't trying to drown myself because of you. I don't even think I was trying to drown myself at all. I needed to think about some things. It doesn't make much sense, and I know that, but I've had a rough night." I scrunched my nose.

"If I wasn't the reason, then what was?" Connor turned his face to me.

"My dad mostly. He left my family when I was seven. He cheated on my mom, and she made him leave, but he never once tried to come back or talk to us until last week. He kept calling and I kept telling him to leave us alone. Then today, he showed up at my house. I left before he saw me, and now here I am."

Connor took my hand. "I'm sorry. I never would have known. And here I was thinking it was all about me." Connor smirked.

"Yeah, you're pretty selfish," I teased.

"What does this all mean for us?" Connor asked.

I stared out the windshield at Jake's house as I considered what I wanted. There had been so much going on, I never stopped to consider what starting anything with Connor might mean. Had I only wanted to use him to get back at Jake? No. But did I want to jump into a new relationship after escaping my last one? Also no.

I sighed and squeezed Connor's hand. "Can we take things slow? Like, do the whole going on dates and getting to know each other thing before we consider being in a relationship? I don't think I'm ready for that yet."

"Okay, fair enough," Connor said, taking his hand from mine and draping his arm along the seat behind me. "Do you want me to bring you home?"

"Yes, please." The thought of being home, curled up in bed, had my body screaming to move. But a second, more pressing issue flashed in my mind: my dad sitting in the kitchen with Clyde. But I had to go home eventually.

Connor started the truck, and we drove to my house. I stared out the window, watching the houses passing by.

A text came through on my phone and I peeked at it.

It was from Jake. *I know everything that happened last night was messed up. But I still love you, Ally.*

Shoving my phone into my pocket, I decided to ignore it for now. The freedom I'd felt from finally ending things with him was too fresh, and exciting. There was no way I'd ever let him back in, but I also wouldn't leave him hanging. I'd respond, at some point.

We pulled into my driveway, and I kissed Connor on the cheek before getting out of the truck.

"Call me, okay?" I said.

"Of course." He smiled.

I waved as he drove away, but I couldn't help thinking that he wouldn't call. If it was Jake, he wouldn't. But Connor wasn't Jake, so maybe he'd keep his word.

Once Connor's truck was out of sight, I glanced over at Zac's driveway. He'd returned home from somewhere and was walking inside. I hurried to catch up with him.

"Hey!" I called after him, and he turned around, looking surprised to see me.

"Hey, you good?" he asked.

I nodded and laughed. "Yeah. Everything's good." It felt weird standing there with him again after so long. It reminded me of life before Jake and how much more carefree I'd been.

"I know this is kind of random, but can we hang out? I miss you." Tears welled up in my eyes as I realized how true that statement was.

Zac smiled. "Of course. Come on."

Chapter Fifteen
Zac

The next day at school, everyone was buzzing with the news. It was like that first day back after Ally's disappearance all over again. Even though it wasn't in the news article, everyone seemed to know that I had been the one to find Ally's body. They stared and whispered when I passed by.

Ignoring them all, I went about my day trying my best not to snap at anyone. My friends didn't ask any questions at lunch, and they acted as if nothing had happened. I didn't know if that was better or worse than dealing with reliving that night.

Now that the police had Ally's body, I figured it wouldn't be long before they were able to determine who had killed her. That fact should bring me relief, but dread coated my insides instead. I still couldn't remember what happened the night she died and couldn't say for certain that I wouldn't be the one they put behind bars in the end.

Though if I had killed Ally, for whatever reason, I deserved to rot in jail.

"Zac," Mariah's voice snapped me back from my inner grumblings. She stood beside me as I stared into my locker.

I cocked my brow and gave her a questioning look.

Placing her hand on my shoulder, she said, "You okay?"

"Not really." I shook my head and swallowed down the grief forming a lump in my throat. "But I will be. Once I figure out how Ally wound up dead and buried behind Aaron's house."

"So, you still don't remember then?" Mariah asked, frowning.

Slamming my locker shut, I walked past Mariah. I didn't have time to debate what I remember and didn't remember with people.

"Zac," Mariah called out to me.

I turned my head back to look at her, and my shoulder slammed into someone, who cursed as something solid hit the ground.

"I'm so sorry," I said, whipping back around. "I-"

Adriane bent down to pick up her book and avoided looking at me but made no move to get away from me as we stood inches from each other. Heat rose to my cheeks and my heart rate kicked into overdrive.

"It's fine," she mumbled and took a step back.

The breath rushed out of me.

"Can we talk? Maybe after school today?" I asked before she could walk away.

She finally lifted her gaze to meet mine. I could see the answer there before she said, "No. I'm not ready yet." Before I let go of hope completely, though, she added, "But I'll text you soon, okay?"

I smiled. "Okay."

That day after school, I went back to the park. Now that Ally's body had been found, I didn't need to wander around the forests anymore, but I did go to the pond in the woods behind the playground, where I had a vague memory of going the night she died.

"Why would we have gone down this path," I muttered as I picked my way down the overgrown, rocky path through the woods.

"I'm going to investigate," Ally said. "You coming?"

Her voice was like an echo in my mind. This time, no images flashed in front of me, only the sound of her voice.

"Investigate what?" I asked, as if the Ally from my memories might hear me and answer.

I kept walking until I reached the opening with the pond in the middle. There was a small dock that was falling apart on the other side of the pond. It wouldn't hold so much as a rabbit.

The wind picked up, sending the leaves on the ground spiraling around me. Branches swayed in the trees above and the birds who remained behind for the winter took flight into the sky.

"I can feel you here," I whispered into the wind. It was almost as if Ally were there with me, standing out of view. The scent of vanilla mixed with coconut wafted through the air. It was Ally's favorite body spray.

Chills brought goosebumps up on my arms and legs, and the cool air seemed to drop another ten degrees.

A scream rattled in my brain that didn't belong to Ally, but I knew it was connected to that night.

"Can you tell me what happened to you?" I asked the wind. Obviously, no response came, but I held my breath for a few seconds as I waited anyway.

Eventually, I had to go home. All the families who had been on the playground when I arrived were gone when I left. I checked my phone, hoping I had a text from Adriane, but there was nothing.

She didn't text the next day either.

I tried my best to not obsess over checking my phone, but there wasn't much else to do since I had resigned myself to the fact that I'd never remember anything else from the night of Ally's death, and I'd have to wait for the police officers to do their job and find her killer.

It was almost a relief to go back to the therapist's office, so I could have an hour where I was distracted enough I didn't need to check my phone.

"Walk me through that day, starting from when you woke up in the morning, to the last things you remember," Dr. Ryan instructed as she jotted something in her notebook.

I started with waking up, taking my daily shower, eating breakfast, and all the other mundane things leading up to spending my night with Ally. Dr. Ryan even had me try to remember everything I ate, what I wore, and any other little details that seemed useless to me.

"We got to the playground, and that's when everything starts to get fuzzy," I said, mentally picturing that moment when my memory turned to black emptiness.

Dr. Ryan tapped her pen against her chin. "Don't push yourself too hard but tell me what you *do* remember."

"Okay." I took a deep breath. "Jake was sitting with some of his friends on a picnic table to the right when we arrived. Mariah came up to us and Ally went with her somewhere. Then I remember being on the top of the tower while Ally was on the swings with Mariah." Closing my eyes, I could imagine the moment vividly, but when I tried to move past that moment, it was like the curtains were drawn and hid the rest from view.

"You said that you had a memory of walking down the path toward the pond, tell me about that."

I cleared my throat. "Right. That." I closed my eyes again. "I was following Ally, I think. She wanted to investigate something. We must have heard something in the woods."

"Josh? What are you doing?" Ally's voice sounded as clear as a bell in my ears.

I opened my eyes and my jaw dropped.

"What is it?" Dr. Ryan prompted.

Why hadn't Josh said anything about being there that night? I'd never explicitly asked him if he had, but I'd think he would tell me something like that, unless...

"I need to go," I said as I stood. My phone rang at the same time, and I glanced at it, shocked to see Adriane's name flash across the screen.

"Zac, please sit," Dr. Ryan said, but I was already halfway to the door.

I turned my head back to look at her. "I'll see you next week."

She shook her head but didn't try to stop me. Once I was outside, I called Adriane back.

"Hey, sorry I missed-"

"Where are you right now?" she asked in a rush.

I glanced around, half expecting her to be waiting for me somewhere in the parking lot. But there were only a few other cars, and no person in sight.

"I just left my therapist's office downtown. I'm headed home now." I hopped in my truck and the engine roared to life as I turned the key in the ignition.

"Don't go home." Adriane's breathing sounded like she'd been running or something.

I put my phone on speaker and placed it in my cupholder as I drove.

"What do you mean? Why shouldn't I go home?" I asked. Someone honked behind me as I hesitated to pull out of the parking lot. Glancing in the rearview mirror, I glared at the person, hoping they could feel my annoyance.

Adriane remained quiet, and I thought she might have hung up, but then she said in a whisper, "The police are on their way there to arrest you."

I almost slammed on the breaks, but at the last second remembered I was in the middle of a busy street and that would end badly. Instead, I lowered my speed to the speed limit and concentrated on not driving off the road as I fought off a panic attack.

"What do you mean? Why are they arresting me?" I managed to get out between gasping breaths.

Buildings blurred in my peripheral vision as I drove. A part of me knew I should pull over, but another part of me wanted to get back into town, regardless of whether the police were looking for me.

"They found some evidence on the body linking you to Ally's murder."

"Why are you telling me this? Why not let them arrest me?"

Another long paused followed before Adriane said, "Because despite whatever they found, I don't believe you did it. Maybe that's stupid, or naïve of me. So be it."

I couldn't help but laugh. "Thank you. I think you're probably one of the only people who thinks that, besides my mom."

"And you," Adriane pressed. "Don't tell me you think *you* did it? Because then I'll really feel stupid."

Even with the new revelation I'd had in therapy, I still couldn't say that I hadn't murdered my best friend. So, I'd have to figure that out before the police found me and put me in a cell.

"I'm going to Josh's house," I said, deciding in that moment that I would confront him about what I'd remembered. With a clear plan, my panic eased. Josh would be able to clear this up, and I could figure out what really happened. At least, that's what I told myself so I wouldn't continue to spiral.

"Why?"

"I think he was there the night Ally was killed. It's a vague memory, so I'm not entirely sure, but I need to talk to him about it." I pulled off onto a side road that would take me to Josh's house.

Adriane let out a little gasp. "You can't go alone! What if *he* killed her?"

I'd had the thought too, but there was no way that Josh was the murderer. "Josh had no reason to kill her. That would be crazy."

"I'm meeting you there. He only lives a few streets over from me."

"That's unnecessary. Josh would never do anything to hurt Ally, or me for that matter. Stay home and stay safe."

"The fact that you want me to stay home proves you might think he could be dangerous too. I'm coming and I'm hanging up now so that you can't keep trying to convince me otherwise. Goodbye!" The phone went silent, and I groaned in frustration.

This was my mess to clean up, and Adriane didn't need to get mixed up in it. Maybe she was right, and I did believe that Josh might be dangerous. He had a bit of a temper, but he'd never hurt anyone that I knew of.

I had to admit, though, I was excited at the idea of hanging out with Adriane again, even if it was only to talk to Josh about Ally's murder. She believed I was innocent, and that meant that I might have a chance with her again.

Focus. I shook my head. This wasn't the time to think about that. I needed to concentrate on the task at hand which was talking with Josh.

His house came into view and panic gripped me. *What if Adriane's right? What if Josh did kill Ally?*

Chapter Sixteen
Alana
October Thirteenth

Since Zac and I had finally made up and were hanging out, we decided we should have one of our Uno nights. He helped me to forget everything that was going on with my dad, who had stopped by again that day to talk with Dianna.

I was packing for Zac's house when my phone chimed. Jake's name lit up on the screen and I groaned.

"What do you want now?" I answered, my annoyance clear in my tone.

"That's nice. I was trying to be civil and invite you to come to the park tonight. There's a group of people going, your friends too," he sounded annoyed too, as usual.

"I kind of have plans," I told him, but it did sound kind of fun. "But if Zac's invited too, I'll come," I compromised.

"Sure, whatever. I should have known you'd already be onto the next guy. Did you at least warn Connor?" he asked sarcastically.

"You know, I don't need this right now. I'll see you tonight." I hung up before he could say anything else.

"Hahaha! I win again!" I threw down my last card on Zac's carpet.

"You cheat." Zac stuck out his tongue at me.

"No way! I'm a champion Uno player!" I giggled and stood. "Come on. Let's go somewhere."

"Where?" Zac stood as well.

"The park?" I suggested.

"All right. We have to be back by nine though, school night and all that."

"That gives us two hours. Let's go!" I pulled him out of his bedroom and out of the house.

"Why do we need to get there so fast?" Zac asked.

I hadn't realized I was practically running down the street. Jake hadn't mentioned Connor being at the park, but I hoped I'd see him.

Slowing down, I turned to Zac and smiled.

"There may or may not be a bunch of other people already there," I admitted.

"Oh, I thought this was, well never mind." His gaze drifted to the leaves on the ground.

"I know it's our night, but this will only be a quick thing, I promise. We can go back to your house at eight if you want." I fluttered my eyelashes at him.

"No, no. It's fine. Nine o'clock is good," he sighed.

I squealed and hugged him.

"You are the BEST friend anyone could have." I meant it when I said it. I caught sight of Mariah on the playground and hurried toward her. "Hey! I was worried Jake was lying when he said my friends would be here," I said.

Mariah rolled her eyes. "I wouldn't have put it past him to lie to you, again. I am so happy you finally ditched him. But how are you?" She took my hands in hers.

"I guess I'm good. It's just weird, you know?" Tears pricked my eyes, and I wiped them away.

"Oh Ally, I know. When Josh and I broke up I had no idea what to do with myself the next day. I didn't have to text anyone good morning or check in with him. I felt free, but also lost. Now things are going back to the way they were before we were ever together."

Realizing that Mariah could help me through this made me feel a little better. As much as I loved spending time with Connor, I was still thick in the grieving process of getting over my relationship with Jake. I didn't miss him as much as I missed the potential of what we could have had, were he not such a horrible boyfriend. It was easier to see the worst of him now that I'd separated myself from him, though sometimes I still yearned for him.

"I don't know if things will go back to normal so easily for me," I said, wrapping my arms around myself.

"Well, I'm here for you every step of the way." Mariah gave me a side hug and leaned her head against mine.

We spent some time on the swings, chatting with some other girls, when I noticed Zac sitting alone at the top of the tower, staring out over the playground. I motioned to Mariah that I was headed up, and we both started climbing.

"Hey Zac, how's it going?" Mariah greeted him and sat beside him.

I sat on the other side of him and slung my arm around his shoulders, leaning my head on him.

"Uh, good, I guess. What are you girls up to?" He seemed suspicious, which made me laugh to myself.

"Nothing, we're just bored down there. You should come mingle with us. There are some interesting people here," Mariah said. We both knew that Zac wasn't friends with any of those people, but Mariah was trying to help him feel more comfortable. She was good at that, and I envied her ease with making others feel welcome or included.

"I think I'm good up here. There is no one down there I want to *mingle* with," he mocked Mariah.

"Oh well, I tried. Come on Ally, let's go back down."

I shrugged and stood to follow Mariah.

"Alana don't go back down there." I turned back as Zac spoke.

"Give me a reason to stay up here." I crossed my arms over my chest and Mariah waited impatiently on the ladder.

"One reason, your best friend, A.K.A. *me*, is up here, and..." Zac hesitated. "And it's supposed to be our night." He closed his eyes and turned to face the front of the tower.

"I know, I know. But we need to live a little, have some fun." God knows I missed out on enough fun while I'd been with Jake. "Come on, Zac, everyone else is down there." I pointed to all the people below the tower. "I'll come back up later. Or you could come down with us." I grinned.

"No thank you." He stood and rested his chin on the railing to stare out into the darkness again.

I took that as our cue to leave.

Once they were on the ground, Jake approached me, and Mariah stiffened.

"What does he want now?" she murmured.

"Hello ladies. How's your night going?" he asked.

I studied his face trying to see if he was scheming, waiting to insult me again like he'd tried to do on the phone.

"It's fine. How's yours?" I decided to stay casual. I wasn't going to give him any reason to go off on me.

"Fine. I noticed Zac doesn't seem to want to be here. Why'd you even bring him?" There it was. He wanted to nag me for hanging out with Zac again.

"Good talk." I walked away before he could say anything else. Mariah followed close behind me.

"You have grown so much! I am so proud of you for walking away from that loser."

I was fuming, but I managed to smile at Mariah. No matter if I was with Jake or not, a habit that was hard to break was wanting to defend him anytime Mariah, or anyone else, talked bad about him. I shoved that feeling down and thought about anything else besides Jake.

Zac climbed down from the tower eventually, and I waved him over.

"Yay! I knew you'd come down from the tower eventually." I hugged him, happy to have a distraction from everyone else. Connor wasn't there, and I regretted my decision to come.

"Yay," he said sarcastically. "I'm not friends with any of these people, Ally."

"Well, you should try to *become* friends with some of them. You're friends with Mariah." I pulled Mariah over to my side from where she'd been talking with Jess.

"I was talking to someone, Alana," Mariah laughed.

"Sorry, but aren't you and Zac friends?" I asked.

"Yeah, why?" Mariah glanced at Zac.

"He says he's not friends with anyone here," I said. Mariah laughed and rolled her eyes, then she turned back to Jess, and they both walked off.

"I think I'm going home. It's almost nine anyway." Zac started walking away.

"No! Please stay!" I pleaded with him. As much as I wanted to leave, I didn't want Jake to think that I'd left early because of him.

"Fine. Where's Jake? I saw you talking with him." Zac glanced around.

"He went for a walk with a couple other people. Hey look! It's..." I was cut off by someone screaming. It was followed by a peal of laughter.

Zac and I both jumped and then burst out laughing.

"Like I was saying, it's Jake!" I dreaded his approach, knowing he had something awful to say, but I tried to stay upbeat for Zac's sake. I wouldn't let Jake ruin my night so easily.

"Hey Ally." Jake ignored Zac's presence. "Why did you walk away from me?"

"Like you don't know," I mumbled. Looping my arm around Zac's I leaned on him for support. "How's your night going, Jake? Having fun?"

"Amazing, actually." His jaw clenched as he stared at where I'd attached myself to Zac. "So glad you two could make it. Have you told Zac about your new boyfriend yet?"

My eyes turned to slits and I could practically feel the steam coming out of my ears.

"I don't have a new boyfriend, Jake," I spat. "Why did you even invite me if you only wanted to fight?"

Zac tugged on my arm. "Come on, let's go. You don't need to deal with this."

Jake laughed. "That's right, walk away."

I broke away from Zac.

"What is your problem? Let me go!" I shoved against Jake's chest, and he stumbled backwards.

Zac stepped between us and tried to steer me away.

"This is between Alana and I, stay out of it," Jake hissed. Zac ignored Jake and only looked at me.

"Let's go Ally."

Jake stormed off, and I let Zac lead me toward the swings.

"I wouldn't have come if I'd known it would be like this," I said, dropping down onto one of the swings. Zac sat on the one beside me.

"I'm sorry he's such an ass."

I opened my mouth to respond, but I stopped when muffled shouting started behind us.

"What do you think that is?" I asked, turning to stare into the woods. There was a path leading to a pond, but otherwise nothing else was in those woods.

Zac shrugged. "Let's ignore it."

I hopped off the swing and walked toward the path.

"I'm going to investigate. You coming?" I smirked and Zac huffed a sigh.

"Yeah. I'm right behind you," he said, following me down the path.

Chapter Seventeen
Zac

I parked on the street a few houses down from Josh's and waited for Adriane. It didn't take long for her to show up, and we met in front of Josh's house, staring up at what I knew to be Josh's window. There were no lights on, which wasn't exactly telling since the sun had only just started to go down.

Taking deep breaths, I bit my lip and steeled myself to walk up to the front door. Adriane took my hand, and we moved forward.

"It won't take long for the police to find you here," Adriane said. "So, we have to make this quick. They know Josh is your closest friend, so they'll come here after they check your house."

"Right." We stopped in front of the door, and I raised my hand to knock. When I hesitated, Adriane knocked for me.

"You've got this."

I held my breath, until I realized no one was going to answer the door. Letting it all out in a huff, I knocked again. Still, no one came to the door.

"What do we do now?" Adriane whispered.

Backing up, I gazed at Josh's house again. I wasn't leaving without answers.

"We go in."

Turning the doorknob, the door opened, and Adriane pushed the door open. "Well, it *is* open." She smirked.

We hurried inside and shut the door behind us before any neighbors would see. Inside, it was dark and quiet. Josh's parents wouldn't think too much of me entering without an invitation, since I'd done it so many times before. But if Josh was truly hiding something, then we'd have to try to make sure he didn't catch us snooping around his house.

"His room is upstairs," I said, heading for the stairs to the right of the entryway. His room was at the end of the hall, next to the bathroom. It was convenient for sneaking out, since there was a trellis leading up to the bathroom window.

Josh's door was open, and I peered in, making sure he wasn't in there, but it was unoccupied. Clothing had been strewn about, and schoolbooks were piled on the desk in the far-left corner. His bedding was all lumped into a pile on the floor beside his twin sized bed in the corner of the room.

"What are we looking for?" Adriane asked, walking over to the desk and picking through some of the books.

Moving to the center of the room, I considered what might hold any kind of answer for me. Josh wasn't one to keep a journal.

"Yeah, what are you looking for?" Josh's voice caught me off guard, and panic made me freeze in place. Adriane faced Josh, but her eyes kept flicking at me.

Right. I came here to talk to him. Turning slowly, I put a smile on my face and tried to act normally.

"I actually came here to talk to you," I said.

Josh wore a scowl as he watched me carefully. His posture was stiff he blocked the entire doorway so if we wanted to leave, we'd have to push past him.

"About what?" he asked, widening his stance and blocking the exit even more thoroughly.

Rubbing the back of my neck, I said, "It's probably nothing, and you're going to have some explanation. But I remembered something from the night Ally died. You were there. At the end of the path, when Ally and I heard yelling and went to investigate, we found *you.* " My memory blocked out who he had been yelling at, or with, but I didn't want Josh to know how much I remembered yet, in case he revealed the pieces I was missing.

Josh's eyes shuttered closed and his hands fisted at his sides. My stomach dropped. He wasn't about to give me a reasonable explanation.

"I really wish you had stayed out of this. Let things be and move on," he said, his head cocking to the side as he opened his eyes. "This could have all been avoided."

Reaching around to his back, he pulled a gun out and pointed it at Adriane.

"Put it down," he said. I turned to see she held her phone in her hand, but she dropped it as soon as Josh told her to. I moved to block her, but Josh growled, "Move and I'll kill you both."

Josh moved toward the bed and grabbed a duffle bag I'd missed when scanning the room. It had blended in with the rest of his clothes and bedding.

My mouth had gone dry. For some reason, Josh had killed Ally, and now he was in a position to kill me or Adriane too. I'd let her come here, thinking she'd be safe, and I failed her like I'd failed Ally.

"Why did you do it?" I asked.

Josh still pointed his gun at Adriane, and I needed to distract him so she could move, or I could, to block her.

Rolling his shoulders, Josh took his eyes off us for a second, so I moved a few inches to the right.

"I didn't." He rubbed his eye with the heel of his palm, his aim wavering and the gun lowered slightly. "You obviously still don't remember *everything.*"

Chapter Eighteen
Alana
October Thirteenth

I stepped over a large branch that laid across the path leading to the pond. The voices became louder, and I recognized Mariah as one of them. *Why is Mariah out here?*

"I'm sorry! I don't want to do this anymore!" Mariah sobbed.

I picked up my pace.

"Where... Josh what are you doing?" Fear spiked Mariah's voice and I ran. Zac lagged and cursed as he tried to keep up.

Breaking free from the undergrowth and trees, I stopped in my tracks. Josh held a gun pointed at Mariah. They both turned to look at me, Mariah's eyes round with fear.

I moved toward her, but Jake ran out of the trees to my right, launching himself at Josh. I threw my arms around Mariah, checking her over to make sure she was all right, and then backed away.

Jake was still struggling with Josh, speaking too low for me to hear what he said.

"Wait, stop!" I cried out. There was too much happening. "Please, no..." I caught Zac exiting the path out of the corner of my eye and yelled to him, "Zac!" Hoping he'd know to get the hell out of there.

A gunshot pierced the air and cold washed over me. A ringing in my ears blocked out all noise. As I fell, I watched Zac slip in the mud as he ran toward me, and fell against a tree, hitting his head on the roots twisted at the bottom.

And everything went black.

Chapter Nineteen
Mariah
October Thirteenth

Tears streamed down my face. Josh gripped my arms and shook me. Jake stood off to the side, his jaw slack. I couldn't help but stare at Alana lying on the ground, blood spreading around her, seeping into the dirt. *She'd save me.*

"Everyone be quiet! Let me think," Jake said. I hadn't realized Josh and I were still arguing. I don't even know what words were coming out of my mouth.

Jake continued. "Josh, get her under control and make sure she doesn't talk. This was an accident. No one meant to kill anyone." Jake was rambling. "God, what do we do? Shit."

Josh walked over to him and shook him like he'd done me.

"Get it together man. I'll take the gun, it's mine anyways. Mariah won't talk, or else." He glared at me for a second and I knew exactly what he meant. He would finish what he had been trying to do earlier before Ally and Jake interrupted. I could have been the one lying on the ground surrounded by a pool of my own blood.

Oh God. I'm the reason Alana's dead. That should have been me. I felt lightheaded and swayed on my feet.

"Someone needs to get Zac out of here." For some reason that was the first thing I thought of. He didn't need to wake up to this sight. I needed to help *someone* tonight.

"Shit, he saw this. We'll never keep him quiet." Jake was hyperventilating, he was almost worse off than me.

I walked over to Zac, still laying on the ground. There was a chance he wouldn't remember what had happened. I needed to believe that, or else he was as dead as Alana.

"He didn't see," I lied, this time glaring at Josh for backup. I hoped that his friendship with Zac might mean something to him. Josh nodded.

"Yeah, he passed out before anything happened. We were out of his line of sight," Josh lied, and I breathed a sigh of relief. "Let's get him up to the playground and leave him there instead." Jake and Josh positioned themselves at Zac's head and feet and hauled him up the path and back to the playground.

"Stay with Alana," Josh shouted back to me. "We have to hide her body."

I gaped at him. I was not going to move her, I couldn't. That was asking too much. But I stayed behind with her until they returned.

After, I went back to the playground, refusing to help them hide the body. I didn't need to know where it was. *They body.* I couldn't think of it as Ally.

They'd laid Zac down at the base of the tower. I walked over to him and noticed his eyes fluttering as if he was trying to wake up.

"Zac, are you all right? You just... Collapsed. I don't know what to do. Please, Zac..." I tried talking to him, but he didn't wake up. Tears streamed down my cheeks.

Wiping my eyes, I left the playground, but quickly realized I couldn't leave Zac there, so I went to the single payphone in our neighborhood, which was next to the park and left an anonymous tip that someone was hurt on the playground.

At least I didn't tell them about Alana, so Josh couldn't be mad about that. Zac was his best friend; he should be worried too. I went home and cried all night, unable to wipe the memory of Alana being shot from my brain. Each time it replayed, I felt as if it were me who'd been shot. And I almost wished it *had* been me.

Chapter Twenty
Zac

As if a veil had been lifted in my mind, all the memories came rushing back in. It wasn't like before, when I would black out and relive them, but they were just *there*. As if I'd never forgotten them.

"It was an accident," I said. "It was an accident, and you didn't mean to kill her. But *you* brought that gun to the pond, didn't you?" I pointed to him. I remember seeing him struggling with Jake, but then the gun fired, and Ally fell... And so, did I. I'd slipped in the mud.

"I can't let this ruin my life," Josh said. "I never would have hurt Mariah, I just meant to scare her. And then Jake came..."

"Jake?" Adriane asked, looking between us.

I glanced back at her. "I'll tell you everything later," I said.

Josh pointed the gun at me. "No, you won't. I'm sorry Zac, but if I let you live, I won't be able to get away."

"You won't be able to get away anyway," Adriane said. "The police are outside." Her gaze went to the window. It led to the backyard, but maybe the police were surrounding the house, if she was telling the truth.

"Don't make this worse for yourself. Let us go, and I'll make sure to tell them that it was an accident. That you never meant to hurt Ally," I tried to reason with Josh.

Without taking his gun off me, Josh went to the window to check Adriane's story. He must have seen something because he dropped his head into his hands, his gun pointing at the ceiling.

Adriane moved to my side, and we backed toward the door. I kept her behind me.

"Wait." Josh lowered his arms. "I have no right to ask this, but will you stay with me until they come? I don't want to be alone."

Turning to Adriane, I gave her a slight nod and she left. I moved slowly over toward Josh, watching the hand he still gripped his gun in. He slumped to the floor, and I sat beside him.

I wasn't sure how to feel about Josh anymore. We'd been best friends, and he'd threatened to kill me not five minutes earlier. He'd threatened to kill Mariah. For the moment, I pushed those thoughts aside and tried to put myself in his shoes.

"Are you scared?" I asked, keeping my voice low. The door downstairs slammed against the wall as if it had been kicked in. Neither of us moved.

Josh set the gun down beside him, out of my reach.

"I don't know what I feel. Numb maybe?" He stared at the floor, pulling his knees to his chest.

Footsteps pounded up the stairs.

We didn't talk anymore, and the police appeared in the doorway, guns trained on Josh. I inched away from him, and they closed in, pulling him to his feet, and handcuffing him.

It all seemed to happen so fast, it was like I blinked, and he was gone. They took Adriane's phone too. Apparently, she'd called her dad before dropping it and he'd heard the whole thing. That's how he'd known to come with the rest of the police force.

It was over.

Chapter Twenty-One
Jake

I'd hoped that the police would give up on finding Alana's killer, but then Zac had to go and find the body. That changed everything. It was only a matter of time before they figured out what had happened. It didn't matter whether it was an accident, or that Josh had brought the gun to the pond in the first place.

I played a role in Alana's death, and I would go away for it. If I'd been more careful when trying to take the gun from Josh, maybe things would have gone differently. *If I hadn't gripped the gun so hard. If I hadn't pulled the trigger.*

My eyes snapped shut as the echo of a gunshot reverberated through my mind. That sound would never leave me.

"Ally…" I took the picture of us I still had on my side table and stared into her eyes. Maybe it hadn't been an accident. Maybe I'd wanted this, in the moment. "I'm sorry," I said, hoping she could hear me wherever she may be now. If there even were an afterlife. I wasn't so sure I believed in that.

I sat on the edge of my bed and waited, wondering when the police would figure it out. *Today? Tomorrow? Next week?*

It turned out to be the next day. I was arrested outside my home with my dad watching, disapprovingly, from the window. He shut the curtains as the police drove me away.

Chapter Twenty-Two
Zac

I waited until the police had left before going outside. Josh had said he felt numb, and I was beginning to feel that too. After weeks of wondering and half-believing myself to be a killer, I felt sucked dry now that it was all over. Everything around me seemed as if it were in a haze and all colors and sounds were duller. Maybe that was what the world was like without Ally in it.

Her death was an accident. Did that make it worse, or better? *An accident.* Something that could have been easily avoided.

"Zac?" Adriane's voice came to me through the haze. I blinked and things seemed to revert to normal.

We were the only two left in front of Josh's house.

"I need to go home," I said. "I need to tell my mom." I wasn't sure why that was the first thing I felt the need to do, but I wanted her to know the truth. She'd never doubted me, but I had.

Adriane walked with me to my truck. "I can come with you. If you want."

I nodded. It was nice to not be alone. I understood why Josh hadn't wanted to be alone either.

The rest of the week went by in that same haze. If I tried to recall any specific details of the days, I couldn't. But I didn't mind the numbness. It was a nice reprieve from grief or anger.

Ally's funeral had been set for that Sunday, and I wasn't sure if I was relieved it was finally happening, or if I was dreading it.

When I woke up from a nap in the afternoon on Saturday, Mariah walked into my room. At first, I didn't react, still half asleep, but my brain finally caught on to the fact that it wasn't normal for Mariah to be in my room.

"What are you doing here?" I asked, rubbing my eyes, thinking it might be a hallucination.

Mariah sat on the edge of my desk.

"We need a distraction. We've all been through a lot," she paused, her throat bobbing. We'd talked briefly about what she'd had to hide all this time, and why she hadn't come to me with the truth. I assumed she still blamed herself for all that had happened, since I also blamed myself.

She continued. "So come downstairs."

I ran my hand through my hair, swinging my legs over the side of my bed and sighed. "There better be food. I'm starving," I joked.

Mariah scrunched her nose and led the way downstairs.

Adriane, Aaron, Michael, Jess, and Connor were in my living room playing video games. At first, I thought it was strange that Connor was there, since he didn't usually hang out with me or my friends, but it actually made sense. Jake had been his best friend, and now he was gone. Connor, like me, had lost Ally and his best friend. As Mariah had said, we all needed something to take our minds off what had happened. He noticed me staring and gave me a small wave.

Mariah waved her hand toward the kitchen where there were five boxes of pizza lining the counter.

"Food, as requested," she teased.

"What's everyone doing here?" I asked, emotion swelling in my throat.

Mom walked around the corner from the kitchen and smiled. "Aaron called for you, but you were sleeping." She held my phone out to me. "So, I answered and said he could bring everyone over."

Aaron held his controller out to me. "Want to play?"

I shook my head. "Thanks. I need some food first." After grabbing a plate and loading it with pizza, I sat beside Adriane on the couch. For the first time since Josh had been arrested, the numbness receded, and true happiness leaked in. My chest ached from the feeling, and I leaned into Adriane.

"Having fun?" I asked, smirking.

She kissed my cheek. "I missed you."

"I missed you, too."

Dad flew in Sunday morning in time for Ally's funeral. I met up with Mariah and Adriane inside the funeral home and we all sat together. The whole thing was as miserable as I'd expected. Mariah went through a whole box of tissues by herself, while I held back my tears. The lump in my throat became increasingly painful as the service went on.

"I need some air," Mariah sniffled once the last person had finished talking.

"Me too. Come on." I took Adriane's hand, and we all snuck outside before the rest of the people filed out the door to head to the graveyard. It was across the street from the funeral home.

"I shouldn't have even bothered with makeup today. I'm sure I look terrible," Mariah managed to get out between sobs and laughter. I pulled her into my arms, hugging her tight.

"You got most of it with the tissues," Adriane said. She reached over my shoulder and wiped a black streak from Mariah's face. "There. Now no one would even know you were crying."

Mariah laughed. "Thanks." She sniffled and I backed away from her, taking Adriane's hand.

"We should go over there," I said, pointing to the graveyard where everyone had congregated. We joined the group but stayed near the back, until it was time to throw the flowers down into the grave.

As I walked up to the hole where the casket was, the tears finally won out and trickled down my cheeks. Dropping that flower into the ground took more out of me than anything else.

When everyone dispersed, I stayed behind with Ally's parents. I'd forgotten that her dad was back in town. He'd shown up shortly before Ally died, but I wasn't sure how long he'd stick around. From what Ally had told me about him, I never thought I'd meet the man who had walked out on his family so many years before.

Dianna sobbed onto Ally's dad's shoulder. He also cried, but I could tell he was trying to hold it together. I knelt beside Ally's tombstone and hung my head.

"Goodbye, Ally. I'm sorry I couldn't save you." I whispered so that Ally's parents wouldn't hear me.

When I stood to walk back to the parking lot, Dianna spoke up. "Zac, wait," she said, her voice hoarse from crying. "I have something." She reached into her purse, pulled out a framed picture, and handed it to me. The picture was taken at Ally's grandparents' camp that we used to go to every summer. I couldn't help but smile at the memory.

"Thank you." I hugged the picture to my chest. Dianna nodded to me before turning back to Ally's grave. I took that as my cue to leave and continued to the parking lot. Mariah and Adriane had both already left.

"Ready to go, sweetie?" Mom put her hand on my shoulder.

Taking one last look back at Ally's grave, I took a deep breath and said, "Ready as I'll ever be."

Holly Huntress

About the Author

Holly Huntress is a self-published author and content creator. She graduated from the University of New England in 2015 with a bachelor's degree in English and has been writing stories since grade school. She is driven by the desire to share her writing with the world and to encourage others to do the same. All her books are currently available on Amazon. If you want to connect with Holly on social media, find her at the handle below!

TikTok & Instagram: @authorhmhuntress OR @authorhollyhuntress (Instagram only)

Reviews for *Haunting Memories* on Amazon, Goodreads, social media or anywhere else you review books are greatly appreciated!

Scan here for updates on future projects and events!

Holly Huntress

More young adult books by Holly Huntress

The Broken Angel Series:
Broken Angel
Condemned Angel
Forsaken Angel

The Unbound Series:
Unbound
Disgraced
Awakened
Ruined

Adult books by H. M. Huntress

Punkintown Road

The Forbidden Waves Series:
Forbidden Waves
Ruthless Tides
Beneath Venomous Sails

The Underworld Duet:
A Demon's Deception